The Eternal Staff

By

Rob Sargeant

Published January 2023

The Eternal Staff

Ultrarunner, Timothy Han, was an hour into a two-hour training trail run in the hills west of Amman, Jordan, when a stray dog joined him. It was friendly, running on the dirt path a couple of yards behind, following him stride for stride for twenty minutes. Grateful for company on the deserted switchback trails, Timothy urged the dog to go faster, "Come on! Good boy." It scurried over boulders and jumped into the lead.

Timothy checked his GPS watch. They would reach the summit soon, just in time to watch the sunset over the Jordan valley. He stopped to take a drink from one of the two soft plastic flasks in his hydration vest.

The dog continued running.

"Boy!" Timothy called out, moving uphill, power-hiking. "Boy!"

He heard a distant bark in reply, followed by a faint yelp. The sound came from a crevasse over the next knoll. There was a cave. In the late evening light, it was too hard to see what was inside. Timothy bent over to get a better look. The dog was stuck at the bottom of the crevasse. It barked several times, jumping, trying to claw its way back up, but the slope was too steep.

Timothy crawled down the sheer rock face. His eyesight adjusted. The stray dog was trapped surrounded by walls of white limestone.

"Come here boy." Timothy fell to his knees, speaking softly, putting out his hand so the dog would approach.

While comforting the dog he spotted a straight wooden branch lying on the cave floor. It looked like it didn't belong there. Timothy picked it up. It was a walking stick about six feet long. He examined it further as he brushed dust off it with his hand. Lettering was engraved down two sides of the almond wood staff. It appeared to be sturdy enough to be put to good use.

Cradling the dog in his left arm, Timothy used the wooden staff as support, set across the mouth of the crevasse, so he could pull himself up and climb out. During the process the dog gratefully licked Timothy's face.

Once the dog had its freedom, it ran off. Timothy watched as it disappeared into the shadows. His gaze fell across the walking stick in his hand. The engravings on it were Hebrew letters.

He held onto the staff as he ran another two-and-a-half miles crossing over the summit to Majed Ali Chalet where a taxi waited. He had to wear his headlamp for the last fifteen minutes as there were no streetlights on the gravel road leading to the chalet.

Timothy used what little Arabic he knew to greet the taxi driver and give him directions to his hotel in Amman. It was a popular resort for foreigners as it had a well-maintained pool, gardens, and spa. The driver recognized the address. Staying there was part of Timothy's recovery plan as the week before he had competed in the Wadi Rum 250 Ultramarathon, five days of running in desert conditions, covering a total of two hundred and fifty kilometers.

The air-conditioning inside the taxi was a welcome relief. The humid evening air and the trail conditions had left Timothy's skin covered with sweat and dust. At the hotel he thanked the taxi driver and left him a good tip.

Anxious to get into a shower, Timothy jogged through the hotel lobby carrying the wooden staff like it was just another part of the equipment he used to train as an ultrarunner. None of the hotel staff seemed to notice it.

Timothy's suite on the fifth floor had a balcony view of the pool, gardens, and hills to the west of Amman. City lights stretched across the horizon to the south.

He entered his room, set the walking stick on the floor in front of the king size bed, went to the spacious glass enclosed shower in the corner of the bathroom, slipped off his running shoes, and turned on the water. He pulled the knob on the faucet, but no water came out. A few seconds later he tried it again. Something came out. It was thicker than water though and red. It was blood. He jumped back, his face and hydration vest covered in blood splatters.

"What?" Frantically he reached out to shut it off.

He tried the bathroom sink. Blood came out of it too. "Huh?"

Just then the hotel fire alarm sounded. Screams came from below. Timothy checked over his suite's balcony. Crowds were gathered on the pool patio. A woman screamed in Arabic while using a white towel to wipe blood off a child. It looked like the water in the pool had turned to blood. The hotel manager was there. He raised his voice, motioning for people to leave.

Timothy made it down to the hotel lobby just as several small groups of people were gathered outside the front door in the lane way. Many other guests were experiencing the same problem with the blood. No one could think of a natural cause for this strange occurrence.

"I can offer you alternate accommodations," the hotel manager explained to the crowd. "Our sister hotel nearby here has vacancies. Please wait for buses. They will shuttle you there. We are so sorry about this," he apologized.

Timothy turned down the offer of a new room. He had a flight booked back to America, scheduled to depart the next day. He decided to check out early and find a room at a hotel near the Queen Alia International Airport.

Timothy had his taxi stop at a carpet shop on the way to the airport. He found a cardboard tube there to store the wooden staff. This would protect it while in transit to America. He dropped the package off at the airport oversize luggage desk along with his large suitcase, checked in for the next day's flight.

While drifting off to sleep at the Amman International Airport Hotel, Timothy remembered that there were Hebrew letters on the walking stick. He made a mental note to find someone who could translate their meaning. *"Maybe it's of some importance?"* Timothy dismissed the thought. *"It's just an old wooden walking stick, probably made by some Bedouin."*

Since Timothy was flying business class, the next morning he took advantage of the complimentary breakfast served in the departure lounge, arriving early. He rarely had more than five hours of sleep at night. It had something to do with his high level of health acquired through being a competitive ultrarunner. No other passengers were around at 6 a.m. so he could help himself to whatever he found on the buffet. He settled for blueberry pancakes, eggs, and coffee.

He had two hours to wait before boarding time, so he caught up on answering the text messages on his smart phone. One was from his wife, Sandra. She wanted to know how his recovery was going after the race. He replied that he was doing fine and mentioned that there was an incident at the resort where he was staying so he had to check-out early. "Water turning into blood – you might see something in the news about it," he typed.

Twenty minutes later Sandra sent a text message back, "There is an article about the blood at the hotel trending in the Middle Eastern news."

#   #   #

Seated in business class at thirty-six-thousand feet, Timothy was relaxed. He enjoyed the glass of chilled pineapple juice and the warmed mixed nuts served by the flight attendant. A bearded man in a gray suit took a seat in the aisle cubicle next to him. He held a book with a yellow and black cover. The title, in black bold letters read, The Eternal Staff. It caught Timothy's attention. The man saw Timothy looking his way and introduced himself as Enoch. He had a slight Middle Eastern accent.

"Hello, Enoch, good to meet you," Timothy replied, reaching out to shake his hand. "Are you traveling for business or pleasure?"

"Business," Enoch said, opening his book, flipping to the page where he had a bookmark.

"Is that a good book?"

"So far. The first two chapters are."

"Is it a story about a wooden staff?"

"Yes. Why?"

"I found a wooden staff yesterday while I was running in the hills west of Amman. What a co-incidence."

"I know," Enoch replied. "You wouldn't happen to know an American fellow named Timothy Han?"

Timothy, shocked, paused before answering. "I am Timothy Han."

"I've been trying to find you."

"What for?"

"I need to tell you something."

"What's that?"

"This plane is going to Boston," Enoch said, "and there's someone there you need to meet."

"No, this is a direct flight to Phoenix, Arizona," Timothy argued. "You must've got on the wrong plane."

Enoch shook his head. "Timothy, when you get to Boston, look for Professor Charles Van Mappen - Harvard University professor of Egyptology," Enoch sounded

8

insistent. He wrote the name on the napkin next to Timothy's drink. "Show him the wooden staff you found."

"What?" Timothy stammered.

The Boeing 787 suddenly experienced some turbulence. Timothy glanced away from Enoch to look out the window. When he turned his head back toward the aisle Enoch was gone.

A flight attendant approached Timothy saying, "Please fasten your seatbelt. Can I get you anything?"

"Did you see the man who was seated here?"

"What man? That seat is unoccupied on this flight."

"He had a black beard and wore a gray suit."

"Sorry," the flight attendant said, looking dismayed. "I haven't seen anyone like that."

The napkin with the hand printed note in blue ink was still on the tray next to Timothy's drink. It clearly read in blue ink: Professor Charles Van Mappen - Harvard University professor of Egyptology.

"Maybe he stopped by to visit from economy class," Timothy explained.

"You could be right," the flight attendant said, smiling, passing him some complementary headphones.

"We will be serving a buffet style lunch in two hours. In the meantime, if you need anything just press the bell."

"Thanks." Timothy reclined his seat, put on his headphones, and selected a movie to watch from the touchscreen display in the back of the seat above his legs.

The next few hours went by peacefully until a commotion began on the plane with the report of one small green frog found in someone's dinner salad. A lady in economy class screamed at the flight attendant like she had just found a poisonous spider. Other passengers soon discovered frogs on the plane of various sizes. Frogs hopped from meal tray to meal tray and down the aisles. Timothy spotted one in business class. It leapt at his head. He swatted it away with his hand. Several passengers ran up and down the aisles attempting to catch the frogs in barf bags.

The head flight attendant took control of the situation as best she could, grabbing the public address microphone. "Please, do not panic! Everyone, stay seated. Remember these are just harmless frogs." She signaled to one of the other stewards to inform the pilots.

After a few minutes, with an emphatic voice, the captain spoke to the passengers over the public address system. "Please remain calm. Stay in your seats. If you need to use the toilets one of the flight attendants will accompany you. Air traffic control were informed of our predicament. We have been advised to land in Boston

Logan International Airport, where alternate transport will be arranged so you can reach your original scheduled destination."

Timothy pulled his smart phone out of the top left pocket of his safari vest. He checked for the Wi-Fi signal on the plane and logged in. He typed a text message to his wife. "I won't be home today. Our plane is diverting to Boston." Before he could type more a frog jumped onto his phone screen hitting the send button. "Would you get out of here frog!" Timothy huffed. He flicked the frog away.

A couple of minutes later Timothy spotted the co-pilot approaching, walking down the aisle. "Is all this necessary?" Timothy asked him.

The co-pilot stopped and leaned closer to Timothy. "Yes," he said, speaking softly, "the plane is over the middle of the Atlantic Ocean. The frogs outnumber the passengers three to one. I was just down in the rear fuselage with a flashlight. It's like they're spontaneously multiplying, emerging from the plane's luggage compartment."

"But they're just frogs."

"If they get into the cockpit the plane could experience electrical problems. We can't take that risk."

"I understand," Timothy said, shaking the co-pilot's hand. "Thanks for looking into the cause."

"The cause remains a mystery. No frogs are listed on the cargo manifest," the co-pilot said, before turning and walking away.

Applause erupted when it was announced by the captain that the plane had begun its descent to the Boston Logan International Airport. The frogs had united the passengers with a common cause. People in first class and economy class were all equally annoyed by the invasion.

Wi-Fi continued to work well on the flight. Passengers were able to inform their families of the emergency landing and the ensuing delay getting to Phoenix.

Timothy ensured his wife by text message that he would be home by Friday. This would give him two days in Boston to sort things out with the mystery of the walking stick. He searched a map application on his smart phone for directions to the Harvard University Museum of Egyptology. It was the most likely place for Professor Charles Van Mappen's office.

Security personnel dressed in light blue coveralls and masks met the passengers as they disembarked from the plane. They were escorted to a quarantine area at the airport along with their luggage to be scanned for a variety of contaminants and diseases that may have been spread by the frogs. The process took hours. While he was waiting Timothy overheard that there was a terrorist plot theory that the frogs were used as a host for some deadly disease. None of the testing done produced positive results. A few people showed they had a common cold virus in their system.

The passengers and their luggage were released from holding and were transported by buses to the domestic departures lounge.

Timothy booked a domestic flight for Friday morning. That way he would have time to find Professor Van Mappen and do a long-distance run with his training partner on Saturday in Arizona.

Several TV reporters and their crews waited outside the luggage claim questioning travelers if they knew anything about the flight forced to make an emergency landing due to frogs.

A short, blond haired, female reporter approached Timothy as he went to secure a taxi. "Sir, were you one of the passengers in quarantine?"

Timothy turned away, pulling his over sized wheeled luggage. The long cardboard tube containing the wooden staff was tucked under his left arm. He ignored the reporter's question.

"Sir?" she continued.

Not wanting to be rude, Timothy stopped. "Yes, I was."

The reporter motioned for her cameraman to get closer. "Hello, I'm Jane Katz from Channel 4 News. Could we ask you a few questions?"

"Sure, I'm Timothy Han."

"How come your flight had to make an emergency landing? Was it because of frogs?"

"Yes," Timothy agreed, "it was."

"How many frogs?"

"My estimate would be in the thousands."

Two other news reporters nearby had their crews direct their cameras and mics toward Timothy. Within seconds he was surrounded.

"Has the airline given you any explanation?" Jane asked.

"No," Timothy replied, "it's a mystery to all of us."

"When did you first notice the frogs?"

Timothy thought for a moment. "It was about four or five hours into the flight, just as they were serving lunch."

"How did the passengers respond?"

"Some panicked," Timothy reflected. "But no one was hurt. The worst harm done was that food and drink service was canceled. After we landed, we were all dehydrated and a little hungrier than usual."

"Thank you," Jane said, "we have what we need." She signaled with her hand for her cameraman to cut and stepped closer to Timothy. "Can I get your cell number, just in case we have more questions?" She passed her smart phone to him so he could type in his contact information. Timothy obliged.

When he was done, Timothy pushed past the other reporters so he could put his luggage in the trunk of a waiting yellow cab. He angled the long cardboard tube to fit it in. "Residence Inn, Tudor Wharf, please," Timothy said, shutting the door, taking a seat in the back.

Within twenty minutes, Timothy was at the hotel across from Paul Revere Park. He had a reservation for two nights there. It wasn't his first time staying at the hotel. Four years prior to this, when he ran the Boston Marathon, he had spent the night there. Subway access was close by. Timothy figured it would be easiest to get to Harvard University that way in the morning. It was less of a hassle than renting a car and trying to navigate the streets of Boston.

Timothy tried to relax on the sofa in his room reviewing his plans for the next day. He would walk to the Charles MGH subway station at eight-thirty and catch the Red Line to Harvard Square. From there, he would walk to the Semitic Museum on campus to try and find Professor Van Mappen as he was instructed to by the stranger on the plane. Hopefully the professor would have an explanation for all the phenomena that he was experiencing.

He felt better after calling his wife to let her know what had happened and what he was planning to do. Sandra said she would check the news to see if his interview at the airport was used. There were stories about the frogs on the plane trending on Twitter.

Timothy was grateful for his wife. After the call he set his smart phone down remembering how much she had helped him over the years to train and perform well in races as an ultrarunner. They first met at the finish area of a hundred-mile event inside a recovery tent where she volunteered as a physiotherapist. Six months later they got married while he was on tour, living out of a camper van. They never did stop to have a real honeymoon as they traveled to race events around the country so Timothy could compete. The memories brought a sense of joy to his heart as he drifted off to sleep.

#   #   #

The next day Timothy found there was a young intern manning the reception desk at the entrance to the Harvard Museum of the Ancient Near East.

"Is Professor Van Mappen's office here?" Timothy inquired.

"No," the intern said, "but you're lucky, he is here today with some students, upstairs in the lab two doors down on the right from the mummy exhibit." The intern passed a glossy pamphlet to Timothy and showed him where it was on the map printed inside the cover.

"Thank-you."

Timothy stopped to read some of the information about the ancient Egyptian artifacts on the second-floor display. He followed the sound of voices to an open lab door.

Professor Van Mappen was inside. He was younger than Timothy had imagined with a full head of thick brown hair and a neatly trimmed beard. He wore a white lab coat and used a pair of tweezers, demonstrating to a group of students the proper technique to use when sorting a pile of clay pottery fragments.

Timothy waited for the professor to finish his lesson. He held the long cardboard tube in his right hand.

"Are you one of my students?" Professor Van Mappen asked Timothy, catching him off guard as he stared at one of the mummy displays.

"No," Timothy answered. "I was told to contact you about this walking stick I found in Amman."

"A walking stick, eh? Who spoke to you?"

"He said his name was Enoch. I never got his last name."

"Enoch. I can't recall ever meeting anyone named Enoch in Amman. An unusual name like that I would remember. I don't believe I know him."

"Well, he knows about you. He said you could explain the origins of this wooden staff," Timothy said, tapping the side of the long cardboard tube.

"You have it with you?"

"Yes."

"Bring it into the lab. I'll have one of my students assess it," Professor Van Mappen said, removing the plastic lid from the tube. He carefully pulled the walking stick out and set it on a light table. Two students watched from the opposite side of the laboratory. In the bright light the Hebrew lettering carved into the wood was more discernible. "I'll get those two to clean this up." He checked his watch. "Time for my coffee break. Care to join me?"

"Sure."

"I'm Charles," Professor Van Mappen spoke as he led Timothy to a break room at the end of the hall. They stopped in front of a kitchenette with a full pot of coffee brewed. "So how did you come into possession of this staff?"

"I found it while rescuing a dog from a cave, southwest of Amman. I was on a training run."

"Help yourself, there's cream in the fridge." Professor Van Mappen smiled, pouring a mug of coffee. "A dog in a cave? Was there anything else there you can remember?"

"The cave walls were flat limestone."

Charles stirred sugar into his coffee, talking. "If I showed you a map, could you point out the location?"

"My watch is equipped with satellite GPS. It should have an exact record of where I stopped," Timothy explained, toggling through the record of dates on his watch. He selected his last run in Amman. A small map of the route flashed onto the watch face.

The professor squinted, reading the compass grid bearings on the watch. He used a pen from his chest pocket to make notes on a pad. "Hmm!" he said. "I know this area. According to oral tradition it's near one of the possible burial sites for Moses."

"Thee Moses?"

"Yes."

"That would explain this weird phenomena."

"What weird phenomena?"

"Water turning into blood at my hotel in Amman. Frogs spontaneously multiplying on my plane flight. That's why we had to make an emergency landing in Boston."

Charles set his half-finished mug of coffee down on the counter. He turned to leave the break room. "You should have started with that information. We can test the wooden staff for dating to see if it is that old."

By lunchtime the test was complete. An intern texted the results to Charles' smart phone as he sat with Timothy in Annenburg Hall. The message alert was absorbed by the cacophonous chatter around them. With its wood paneled walls and stain glassed windows the dining room had the same acoustics as a cathedral.

A few minutes later the professor took a break from eating his pasta salad to check his phone. The walking stick was as ancient as he suspected, dated to around 1200 BCE. "Testing shows the staff to be over three and a half thousand years old," he said, passing his phone to Timothy, showing him the message. "See."

Timothy read the document. His heart raced. "Could it be the actual staff that Moses used?"

"As you can read, the Hebrew writing engraved into wood is worn and hard to decipher. One side of the staff has a row of twelve letters, one for each of the tribes of Israel. The side, opposite it, has a row of ten letters, one for each of the ten commandments. And with the strange phenomena that's been occurring around it, the odds are great that this is indeed the staff that Moses carried."

"I found Moses' staff," Timothy laughed in disbelief. "I always thought those stories were just myths."

"The Bible is one of the most historically accurate documents known to mankind. Many secular writers throughout history have confirmed the truths found in it. And now, Timothy Han, you have just become part of that history."

While talking, Timothy used a plastic fork to pick at the pile of French fries on the plate in front of him. "So, what happens now?"

"We'll publish our findings. In the meantime, we can put the wooden staff on display in the old Semitic Museum. We rotate some of the exhibits on a monthly basis."

Timothy was excited by the idea, but he had a question. "Will it be safe?"

Charles nodded, saying, "We have many priceless ancient items at the museum. The security systems there are some of the most modern available. There are double key locks for the vaults and password-controlled alarms."

"But considering the strange phenomena, will it be safe for the museum?"

"I think the walking stick will like its new home here," Charles said. "That man you met on the plane,

Enoch, didn't he tell you to bring it to me?"

"Yes."

"Then don't worry."

#   #   #

Back at his hotel in the evening, Timothy took advantage of the cool spring temperatures to do a training run. Leaving through the front lobby he set out at an easy pace crossing the Charles River, following the harbor walk path, a network of boardwalks that led along beside the water. He thought about the incredible day he had had. It was beyond what he could have imagined. The idea that the God who created the universe was behind the water turning into blood and the frogs on the plane brought a smile to Timothy's face. He couldn't understand it. It was more than he could fathom. But if this was true, other claims made about God's power manifesting throughout history could be true too.

He stopped at Commercial Street to use the base of a streetlight to do some dynamic stretches, swinging one leg at a time to loosen up his hips.

He thought about the wooden staff safely locked in a vault at the Harvard Museum of the Ancient Near East. Professor Charles Van Mappen planned to invite the press to its unveiling at the museum Thursday morning, the next day. E-mailed invitations were already sent out. Charles had no qualms about sharing the find with the world. Timothy wasn't so sure it was a good idea, but he trusted Charle's judgment since he was a highly regarded professor at Harvard.

The out and back training run took about two hours. The sun had set by the time that Timothy returned to the hotel.

At nine-thirty in the morning, the next day, Timothy arrived at the Harvard Museum of the Ancient Near East just as another TV news van pulled up to the curb at the side of the building. There were four already parked there. Production assistants near them unpacked Pelican cases, setting out light stands and tripods. Extra security guards manned the main door, checking IDs as a line-up of people entered. Timothy showed them the e-mailed invitation he had saved on his smart phone.

The press conference was downstairs in a large hall. At the far end there was a podium on a raised platform. Professor Van Mappen was there with one of his assistants standing in front of a glass enclosed cabinet shrouded by a red silk cloth. Timothy went to greet him.

"There seems to be a lot of excitement about your find," the professor said.

"Yes," Timothy sighed, "I never thought I'd ever be part of something like this."

"The Department of Antiquities in Jordan has agreed to work with us. Under UNESCO there are bilateral antiquities agreements between Jordan and America. They will allow us to jointly exhibit the staff of Moses through some of the most prestigious Museums in the world," Professor Van Mappen leaned closer to Timothy, speaking in a whisper, "… and there might be a finder's fee for you, a small percentage."

There was a seat reserved for Timothy on the platform. Ten minutes before the event was to begin, he sat down there next to Professor Van Mappen. The room was packed. Along with several hundred Harvard staff and students were forty-five journalists and TV reporters crammed into the basement hall. Timothy raised his right hand to shield his eyes and squinted into the bright studio lights pointed in their direction. He scanned the crowd of journalists and did recognize one person. It was Jane Katz from Channel 4 News, seated in the second row. She waved at him. Timothy smiled and bowed his head.

Professor Van Mappen was quickly introduced by senior staff at Harvard University. He stood and stepped behind the podium, glancing down at his computer tablet from time to time, reading his notes. "Thank-you all for joining us today. None of this would be possible had it not been for the alertness of this young man here, Timothy Han," the professor started. "He discovered this archaeological object a few days ago outside Amman, Jordan, in an area where for centuries archaeologists have been searching for the burial place of Moses. Possibly, because of recent flooding the location of this ancient artifact was exposed, providing him access. Inside a small cave he found what we believe is Moses' staff." Professor Van Mappen paused and turned away to pull the red silk cloth off the glass enclosed cabinet. Once revealed, the wooden staff seemed to glow inside the display, laid out on a white diagonal panel. The professor's assistants had cleaned it up nicely.

A flurry of beeps, buzzes and flashes rose from the digital cameras used by the crowd of journalists.

Professor Van Mappen motioned for Timothy to join him at the podium. "Do you have any questions for Timothy Han?" he asked the press.

Hands went up all over the room. Timothy stood and joined the professor behind the microphones, pointing to Jane Katz.

Jane was ready with several questions. "How did you come to find the walking stick in Amman?"

Timothy took a quick drink of water and spoke, saying, "I was on a training run in the trails southwest of Amman. A stray dog joined me running along side me for about ½ an hour. The dog led me to the wooden staff when it got trapped in a cavern. I found the staff when I rescued the dog." Timothy continued, "It was a sandy colored Canaan dog."

Jane asked, "Is there a connection between the walking stick and the frog infestation that occurred on a plane that had to make an emergency landing two days ago at Boston Logan International Airport?"

"Yes," Timothy said. "I was on that flight and had the staff stowed with the luggage."

"Were you staying at the resort in Amman that had its water supply turned into blood?"

"Yes, I was there. It was the same day I found the walking stick."

"And you brought it back with you to the hotel?"

"Yes, I thought it was just a walking stick. I didn't realize it was ancient."

Jane Katz sat down. "Thank-you!"

Timothy pointed to a male journalist in the front row, who introduced himself as Tom Santos of Channel 7 News. "This question is for Professor Van Mappen. Sir, what makes you so certain that this is the wooden staff Moses used?"

"Hmm," Professor Van Mappen sighed, itching the tip of his beard with his right hand. "We will soon publish a detailed paper on our findings that will detail why we are so certain that this is the Moses' staff. I'm sure it will be scrutinized by my colleagues and archaeologists across the globe. The most convincing factors are the location where it was found, the engravings on the wood, and the strange phenomena that we're seeing associated with the staff. These convinced me of its authenticity."

"So, you believe the God who led Israel out of Egypt approximately 3300 years ago is the same one who is causing these strange events?"

Professor Van Mappen paused to think before answering. He did believe it. "Yes, I do," he said.

Tom Santos did not seem persuaded. "When will the public be able to see the staff?"

"For the next month it will be on display here at the Harvard Museum of the Ancient Near East (the old Semitic Museum). Following that, exhibits will be at the Penn Museum and the National Archaeological Museum of Amman. There are more venues interested but no dates have been set at this time." Professor Van Mappen's announcement was interrupted by applause from the Harvard University staff and students gathered in the hall.

A few more questions from the journalists were answered by the professor before a representative for the University graciously dismissed the crowd.

A reception in the museum's main floor lobby followed the press conference. Finger foods and refreshments were served by catering staff dressed in matching black suits. Timothy was inundated with questions from the attendees. As an elite ultrarunner he had grown accustomed to dealing with journalists and sports fans. Though it was a different crowd than he was used to he stayed polite and answered queries as truthfully as he could.

At one point Jane Katz asked him if he was a man of faith. Timothy had to think. "I remember my grandmother took me to Sunday School when I was little. Through high school and college, I wasn't involved in any religion. Sports were my thing. Cross country and track. But now, after this …"

Jane interrupted Timothy, saying, "… after this you believe?"

"Yes. I do," Timothy admitted. "There's no other explanation for what I've experienced."

"It is amazing, isn't it?" Jane mused. "Well, I've got to get back to the studio and help with the edit. You're flying back to Phoenix tomorrow?"

"That's the plan. I hope to be home for dinner."

As Timothy helped himself to a glass of punch from a refreshment table, he recognized Enoch in the crowd.

"Enoch!" Timothy called to him, "Enoch!"

Enoch, dressed in a tuxedo, smiled, and approached Timothy, saying, "How are you?"

"Good, what a surprise to see you."

"Yes, I found out about this at the last minute. I'm a little overdressed."

"No. You look good. The last time we talked it was like you vanished into thin air."

"I have to tell you something."

"What?"

"It's important," Enoch continued. "There's a reason why you found Moses' walking stick at this time."

"What's the reason?"

"There's a new Exodus on the horizon."

"A new Exodus?" Timothy asked, taking the last gulp of punch from his glass.

"Yes. And there will be many who will oppose it. But stay strong and don't let them take control of the wooden staff," Enoch said, stepping behind a pillar as they walked. He stopped in front of an alcove bench. "Watch for the signs."

"Timothy," Professor Van Mappen interrupted them, "there's someone here I would like you to meet, Marjan."

Timothy spun around to find the professor with one arm around his wife's shoulder. She wore a black suit dress and a pearl necklace. He recognized her from one of the photos Professor Van Mappen kept in the laboratory. "Marjan, good to meet you." For a few minutes they exchanged pleasantries, reflecting on how well the press conference was received. Later, when Timothy turned back to where Enoch stood, Enoch was gone.

Before returning to his hotel Timothy went down to the museum's basement hall to see the walking stick one more time. Apart from two security guards, one at each entrance and exit, he was alone. Standing next to the glass enclosed display cabinet, Timothy checked to make sure it was secure. He saw that small, red light, laser motion sensors emitted from each corner. The glass was thick looking, like it was bullet proof. He left, confident that Moses' staff would be safe.

#   #   #

Two days later, on the hills of South Mountain Trail outside of Phoenix, Arizona, running a few paces behind his training partner, Matt Carling, Timothy should have felt at home. The familiar terrain, with its boulders and cacti was easy to navigate. Throughout the years he had spent hundreds of days running there. Something had changed. He thought about this as he ran.

Timothy hoped the long run would be a relief from the previous day's stress. National press was waiting for him when he arrived at the Phoenix Sky Harbor International Airport on Friday afternoon. They drilled him with questions about the wooden staff. It took Timothy three hours to get home and he only lived a half an hour away. Moses' staff and the related phenomena that accompanied it was the top news story for most networks that night. Opinions about it were split like the political views of the various states. Timothy just wanted to think about the next stride he was running on the trails of South Mountain Trail, that he would land on stable ground.

The warmth of the rising sun hit the pair as they crossed the summit and headed down the narrow switchback trail toward Hidden Valley. They stopped on the summit after the next assent to take in some carbohydrates. Timothy had a chocolate flavored gel tucked into the front pocket of his hydration vest.

"So much has changed since I was last out here," Timothy sighed, tearing off the top of a gel packet.

Matt looked at Timothy quizzically. "The trails?"

"No, the trails are the same," Timothy replied. "It's my life."

Matt finished eating a chocolate gel. He swallowed and spoke. "You've been a celebrity for years."

"This is different. I don't see the world the same way as I used to now that God is part of my life."

"How do you see it now?"

"Before I found the staff, life was all about what I could make of it through my own discipline and my sheer will power. Now I see I need God's help."

"I understand."

Timothy crumpled the emptied gel pack he held into a ball and stuffed it into one of the pockets on his vest. "And the strange thing about it is, he needs me too," he continued. "It's like I was chosen to find the staff."

Four hours later they were done the training run at South Mountain Trail, having completed almost thirty miles. Timothy was glad they had finished early before the heat under the midday sun made it difficult to run outdoors.

Heat was one of the main reasons they went up to Flagstaff every year, usually in May. He and his wife Sandra owned a two-storey a-frame cabin in the woods at the edge of the city. It wasn't fancy. The cabin had everything they needed, even an extra room Sandra utilized as an office as she did physiotherapy as a profession.

The media frenzy surrounding Timothy and the old walking stick died down after two weeks, just before they packed up and left for Flagstaff. During this time Professor Charles Van Mappen contacted Timothy through text messages each week, giving him updates on the status of the exhibit at the Harvard Museum of the Ancient Near East. He let him know that his first finder's fee was on the way in the mail, a cheque for five thousand dollars. Timothy thanked him, and said he was praying for the success of the exhibits. This was true. Timothy had become a praying man. He prayed in the morning, at night, and while he ran alone for hours training on the trails. He prayed because he knew God was listening.

A week after their return to Flagstaff Timothy went for a long training run in the nearby San Francisco Peaks. He brought along his pocket Bible and lunch in the back pouch of his hydration vest. Following a winding trail through the short pine tree forests and aspen groves he headed up the south face. He took his first break to rest in a meadow where he sat on a log and ate half a peanut butter and jelly sandwich. Reading his Bible, turning to the book of Exodus, scanning for verses about Moses, Timothy wrestled with thoughts. If the Bible was all true, he had to accept it by faith. This included both testaments, the testimonies of Christ's disciples too, and their teaching. He set his Bible down on the log and fell to his knees, humbling himself.

"I can't wrap my mind around this. It's too much to understand," he prayed. "But I accept it as the truth." He waited, listening to the wind in the trees and the distant sounds of birds calling to each other. The air had a chill in it that day. At an altitude of over seven thousand feet, it was common in the Spring. The thin windbreaker Timothy wore kept him warm while he was moving but was ineffective once he stopped. Strangely, as he knelt by the log praying, he felt like a warm blanket was placed over his shoulders. The chill left. Peace came upon him.

The smart phone in his front vest pocket suddenly vibrated. It was Sandra. Timothy swiped the screen open accepting the call. "Hello!"

"Timothy," Sandra said, an anxious tone in her voice, "the FBI are here. They want to talk to you."

"Well, put them on the phone."

"No, they want to question you in person."

"Why?"

"It's something to do with Moses' staff," Sandra said. "It's been stolen."

"Stolen?" Timothy replied. "Give me an hour. I'll meet them at the Humphrey's Trail head on North Snow Bowl Road."

A text message from Professor Charles Van Mappen popped up on Timothy's smart phone screen. He had sent it twenty minutes before the phone call. It confirmed the news of the wooden staff's theft. The vehicle transporting it to Penn Museum was stolen. "They've found the cube van abandoned at a freeway rest stop. Its cargo is gone."

Timothy ran at race pace back to the trail head. It took him about fifty minutes to get back to the parking lot where he found three identical blue sedans parked next to his SUV. A man dressed in jeans, and a long-sleeved khaki cargo shirt, greeted Timothy.

"Hi, I'm Thomas Bright, FBI," he said, flashing his identification card. "Your wife said you'd meet us here."

"She said Moses' staff was stolen," Timothy sighed, catching his breath, doing some cool down stretches.

"Yes, Professor Charles Van Mappen said you might be able to help us locate it."

"How's that?"

"The professor says you have a supernatural connection to it. You've experienced firsthand the strange phenomena that occurs around Moses' staff."

"Do you have any idea of who's behind the theft?" Timothy asked.

"Not currently. They seem highly organized," Thomas replied, describing how the original drivers of the cube van were left bound at the side of the highway, and how its contents were stolen. "We have a business jet waiting for us at Flagstaff Pulliam Airport. We want you to join us. We need your help."

"When are you leaving?"

"As soon as you can be ready."

Timothy felt confident he could serve them. But he did have one request. "I'd like to bring my wife along too, if that's not a problem," he asked.

Thomas checked a notification on his smart phone. "That won't be a problem," he replied.

#   #   #

Two hours later, on the tarmac of Flagstaff Pulliam Airport, a gray Gulfstream G-550 prepared for departure. A rental car shuttle bus drove up to it, stopping fifty meters from the plane's main entrance door, which had its hydraulic folding stairway with handrails fully extended. Timothy and Sandra, carrying luggage, exited the bus. They were followed by the FBI agents.

A flight attendant welcomed the couple, taking their bags, directing them to enter. "Thank-you!" Timothy shouted, to be heard over the whine of the running auxiliary power unit.

The interior of the jet was modified to include computer workstations with racks of several high-definition monitors. Comfortable leather seating, a kitchenette, and a small lavatory took up the rest of the space. Timothy and

Sandra were led to a section where four people could sit facing each other. As soon as the plane reached cruising altitude Thomas came and sat across from them. He opened a laptop and turned it toward them so they could see the screen.

"I'll bring you up to speed," Thomas began, "Here are some photos of the stolen cube van. The strange thing about it are these round dints. The van is covered with them." He clicked through a series of photos. Some showed angles of a smashed windshield. "What did this?"

"I've never seen anything like that," Timothy answered.

"What size are the dints?" Sandra asked, leaning closer to look.

"Five to six inches," Thomas replied, selecting a file that showed a measuring tape next to the damage. "See."

Timothy added, "That's about the size of a soft-ball."

"Could be hail," Sandra suggested. "Was the ground wet around the van? Were there any reports of a storm in the area?"

Thomas searched through past weather reports from the region. "There was a freak hailstorm that came out of no where," Thomas read the news headline flashed across his computer screen. "Hail the size of a soft-ball."

"That was one of the plagues ancient Egypt suffered," Timothy said to Thomas, "Have the FBI search for vehicles with hail damage in the state. The get-away vehicle will probably have damage too."

Thomas agreed, "Good idea!" He spoke and typed, preparing an e-mail that he would send to agents heading to College Township, Pennsylvania, near to where the stolen cube van was found.

Timothy stared out the window next to his seat, thinking. The plane was above the clouds. He suddenly remembered Enoch's words, follow the signs. "We need to follow the signs," Timothy blurted out.

Thomas looked up from his keyboard. "What signs?" he asked.

"The signs of Moses' staff; the plagues. Enoch warned me that someone wanted to take control of the staff."

"Enoch?"

"Yes."

"Who's Enoch? How can we contact him?"

"I don't know," Timothy shrugged. "He just shows

up. He was at the Harvard Museum press conference. The first time I met him was on the plane flight from Amman."

Sandra added, "So, if we do what Enoch said, and follow the signs, they should lead us to the staff."

"I'll let my research team know," Thomas said as he typed out a new e-mail. "Look for unusual occurrences with blood, frogs, flies, hail, boils, locusts, darkness, and death of the first born." Thomas turned to Sandra, saying, "I hope we can get the staff back before that happens."

Three hours later their Gulfstream landed at University Park Airport in State College, Pennsylvania. Its passengers were picked up by a motorcade of blue sedans and taken to the cube van at the I-80 Rest Area. The crime scene was cordoned off with yellow caution tape.

"Put these on," Thomas said, passing Sandra and Timothy each a pair of blue nitrile gloves. "Video surveillance showed the van entering the parking lot. Unfortunately, a transport truck blocked the camera's view of the walking stick when it was transferred to another vehicle." Thomas described the video in more detail as he escorted Sandra and Timothy to the van that was riddled with pock marks caused by the hail.

They walked around the parking lot nearby the van, searching the pavement for debris. After a few minutes Timothy noticed a black ball point pen that was wedged into a crack between the joint of two concrete slabs.

Wearing rubber gloves, he used a twig to pry the pen out enough so he could grab it. It was a complimentary one from a popular hotel chain. He handed the evidence to Thomas, saying, "I have a feeling this will help."

"You could be right," Thomas said, as he read the hotel name printed in white letters on the pen's casing. "But those hotels are in every state."

Thomas gingerly placed the pen in a plastic evidence bag. He passed it to his assistant, telling her to track down the hotels that offered that pen style.

"Were there any witnesses here?" Timothy asked Thomas.

"We've found a state employee who was trimming branches from the trees near the picnic area, he said he saw a brown RV leave soon after the cube van arrived. It had some hail damage."

Timothy thought for a moment and told Thomas, "There's someone I met who could help us. Jane Katz from Boston Channel 4 News, she might be able to help us find this RV."

Thomas mulled over the idea, saying, "Maybe you're right. The press hasn't been informed yet of the wooden staff's theft. We could limit the wanted press release to a hail damaged brown RV and exclude the news of the missing staff."

Timothy nodded. "I have a feeling you'll be able to trust Jane Katz."

Two FBI administration assistants were tasked with the press release giving Jane Katz the exclusive right to broadcast the news.

#   #   #

A temporary mission control was set up at a College Township roadside diner where the FBI agents and their support staff gathered to wait for feedback from the news syndicates. All tips they received were read through there. After two hours of analyzing the information, the consensus seemed to be that the RV was heading toward New York city on highway 80. A helicopter was dispatched to physically locate it.

As they waited, Timothy drank two cups of coffee at a booth with cushioned seats sitting across from Sandra. He tried a couple of the desserts. With a boost of carbohydrates in his system Timothy felt like stepping outside for a long run. Instead, he called Jane Katz to thank her for her help in getting the news out.

A laptop on the table in front of Thomas showed the helicopter's live video feed as it flew over highway 80 in a race against time as less than two hours of daylight remained. The traffic was bumper to bumper at interchanges. Timothy took Sandra's hand and prayed quietly, "God, help us to locate the RV."

Over Stroudsburg the helicopter left the air above the freeway heading toward a strip mall with a huge superstore at its east end. Circling over the parking lot, focusing on an area where six RVs were stopped, the helicopter moved in closer. One of them was brown and dinted. An empty car trailer was attached to its hitch. "I think this is the one," Thomas said, typing out directions for the pursuit vehicles, which were miles away from Stroudsburg on highway 80.

The spotlight on the helicopter turned on as two agents repelled down from its open door. They wore black tac vests and had semi-automatic rifles strapped across their backs. Once on the pavement they went to secure the brown RV. It had no human occupants. The agents quickly exited the RV waving their arms, swatting at something in the air. They looked up to the helicopter, talking on radio headsets.

"Is Moses' staff there?" Timothy asked Thomas.

"They're checking now," Thomas answered. He could barely hear the radio chatter through the video feed. "No. No. It's gone. But they did find signs that it was there."

"What?"

Thomas was amused. "Flies. Swarms of black flies, and piles of dead ones. They're everywhere, the RV's filled with them," he said.

The video feed continued, showing local press who beat the FBI pursuit vehicles to the crime scene. Spotlights, tripods, and cameras were set up, waiting for comments from the FBI. The RV wasn't properly parked. It looked as though its passengers had left in haste. The car trailer attached to it was empty.

"Looks like we'll be spending the night in College Township," Thomas told Timothy and Sandra. "My team's been working for over 48 hours. There's a motel two blocks down the street where everyone's staying."

After midnight Timothy found himself wide awake in their motel room. He decided to go for a run in the deserted city streets, leaving a handwritten note on the desk for his wife who was fast asleep. He headed out, listening to the squeaky sound his shoes made as he ran across the rain-washed pavement, hoping to complete a two-hour tempo run.

Passing street after street of three storey brick buildings, many with small businesses on the main floors, Timothy eventually reached the main College campus for Penn State. There, the streetlights illuminated the deciduous tree lined streets enough that he didn't need to use his headlamp.

As he ran, he thought about the thousands of students attending the University there, students with a will to learn. They could go on to become doctors, archaeologists, anthropologists, and professors. Though the will power of mankind had helped many to accomplish great things through people like this, Timothy realized as he ran that the greatest power in existence was the will power of God. If people would just surrender to it, they could achieve even greater things. Timothy raised his arms as he ran in a symbol of his own surrender. "God, I need you," he called out, "Let your kingdom come. Let your will be done."

Before sunrise Timothy had made it back to the motel room. Sandra was still asleep. She woke up as he showered. Just as Timothy finished dressing for the day, she had a pot of coffee brewed for them to share.

Pulling back the motel window curtains Timothy saw the FBI agents standing around their convoy of vehicles in the motel parking lot. He sipped his coffee.

"Looks like they're ready to go," Timothy said.

"I'll be a second," Sandra called out as she brushed her hair in the bathroom.

A few minutes later, when Timothy and Sandra took their luggage outside, they were met by Thomas who had good news. The ballpoint pen that Timothy found at the rest stop the day before was traced to New York City. A group of hotels there offered them to guests. They also offer free shuttle service for ocean cruise lines. The FBI had growing evidence that the thieves had entered the USA through New York and that they would depart the same way. Radio chatter seemed to indicate that they want to smuggle the wooden staff out of the country on a transatlantic ocean cruise ship. "You both have valid passports with you?" Thomas asked.

"Yes, we do," Timothy and Sandra said in unison as they took seats in the back of the lead blue sedan.

An agent next to them had a bag of fast-food on his lap and asked, "Are you hungry?"

After Timothy's early morning run, he was. "Yes," he said.

"I've got bacon and eggs or ham and eggs."

Timothy chose the bacon and egg sandwich.

Thomas, in the driver's seat, turned the car right onto the I-80, speeding up, merging with traffic. "We should be in New York City in five hours," he said as he peeled the cardboard top off a breakfast burrito using the steering wheel for support.

"Why didn't you tell me you had burritos?" Timothy complained.

Thomas laughed. "Burritos are only for senior staff."

Timothy took two bites of his breakfast sandwich, swallowed, and asked, "So, do you know what cruise ship they're trying to use to smuggle out the staff?"

Thomas bowed his head and replied, "We're certain that it's a Norwegian ship scheduled to leave New York in two days. They chose it because it has over four thousand passengers. We would never be able to vet that amount of people in such a short time frame, especially when they're using fake identification."

"Do you have any suspects?"

"A private fine art auction is scheduled to take place on this voyage. It's known to attract some of the wealthiest investors in the world, a few of them have connections in the black market. They might be involved," Thomas explained. "We were able to get cruise tickets for myself, you, and two other agents."

Sandra was excited by this development. "Really?" she sighed, "I've never been on a cruise ship."

"Inside cabins were all we could manage. They're close to the ship's infirmary on deck thirteen."

"I was wondering," Timothy asked Thomas, "if the ship has a jogging track?"

"Yes, on deck seventeen. There's also tread mills in the ship's gym. You'll be able to continue your training."

"Good," Timothy said, and ate the last bite of his

breakfast sandwich. "I've got a big race next month, a hundred-mile mountain race."

The motorcade of FBI vehicles entered New York City early in the afternoon, avoiding the heavy rush hour traffic that often clogged the streets. They had reservations at a hotel near the Manhattan Cruise Terminal where their ship was moored.

From the window of their hotel suite Timothy and Sandra could look down to see the cruise ship they would board the next day. It was one of three that were berthed at the terminal along the Hudson River. At the pier long lines of semi trucks delivered supplies to the ships. Timothy scanned the horizon as the evening sun settled on the distant skyscrapers. The streetlights and car headlights on the network of New York City streets became more noticeable. To know that the walking stick they were looking for was somewhere amid the vast metropolis, Timothy felt overwhelmed. "It's going to take a miracle for us to find the staff," Timothy sighed.

Sandra took Timothy's hand and patted it, saying, "God's with us. He'll help us."

#   #   #

The day of their departure was mostly spent waiting in lines, lines for a shuttle bus, lines to check-in luggage and lines for ticket and passport control. It was late in the afternoon when Timothy and Sandra found their cabin within the catacomb of hallways on deck thirteen.

Timothy tried to enjoy the experience but was distracted, looking upon the other passengers he passed with suspicion, wondering if they could be the thieves.

The night life aboard the cruise ship had a festival atmosphere with live musical shows in the main atrium's band stand and dancing under the stars by the pools. Timothy and Sandra joined the crowd standing on deck twenty as they passed the Statue of Liberty heading out of the Hudson River to the Atlantic.

At dinner in the Italian restaurant lounge Thomas told Sandra and Timothy about how he had followed a couple through the ship earlier that day. "The husband carried a long black plastic document tube on board with his luggage. My assistant followed them up the elevator to the eighth floor. I intercepted them there before they got to their cabin."

"Did they show you what was inside the tube?" Sandra asked.

"Yes," Thomas laughed, "it was his favourite fishing pole. He took it out and showed me. He wants to go fishing at one of the ports once we reach the Mediterranean."

"So, what's the plan? How're we going to find the staff?" Timothy asked.

"Since you two have a cabin near the ship's infirmary see if you can find out if any passengers are experiencing any strange physical ailments that might be plague related. Sandra is a registered physical therapist. This might open some doors there for her with the nurses."

During his spare time reclining on a deck chair or in their cabin before sleep, Timothy read the Bible. It was the first time in his life that he was able to complete full chapters in one sitting. Reading about the prophets of old like Moses, Elijah, and Daniel, he came to a better understanding of the covenant God made with mankind. Out of love, God took the initiative. He chose to reveal his will to fallible men and use them to fulfill his plans. It gave Timothy hope that he could be used if he trusted in the words of God like those prophets did.

The next lead came two days later while Timothy trained on the jogging track. It was early in the morning, just after sunrise. The cruise ship was moored on the wharf at the Royal Naval Dockyard in Bermuda. The only other runner on the track was a man with a salt and pepper beard and crew cut hair. He spoke with a Middle Eastern accent, introducing himself as Zachary Osman when they stopped to use the drinking fountain.

They ran a couple of laps together chatting about how they were enjoying the cruise. Timothy mentioned that he was disappointed with the fine art auction as he was not a collector of paintings. "I'm interested in acquiring antiquities."

Zachary replied, "I've done this cruise four times and have seen a lot of Bermuda. There's an antique shop in Hamilton. It's not far from here."

"Really. How far?"

"Fifteen minutes by ferry."

"Do they have auctions?"

Zachary smiled, saying, "They do. I bought a grandfather clock there."

"So, they buy and sell antiquities?"

"Yes."

"Thank-you Zachary, my wife and I will check it out," Timothy said as he sped up to complete another set of race pace intervals.

At breakfast, an hour later, Timothy, Sandra, Thomas and two other agents, made plans to go ashore. Hundreds of passengers disembarked that day to explore the beaches and shops near the port.

Timothy and Sandra stepped onto the pier dressed in running gear with the goal of completing a good portion of the twenty-two-mile Bermuda Railway Trail. They planned to meet up with Thomas at the Hamilton antique shop three hours later.

They ran side by side at a pace that would allow them to converse. With clouds overhead, pleasant morning temperatures, and the scent of the lush foliage, the island visit was a welcome change. Passing under roadside palm trees Sandra remarked that it was like a real honeymoon.

After running three miles they came to a residential neighborhood. Following signs to the Somerset Bus Terminal, they found the start of the Railway Trail. The first few miles of the level path were carved through rocky outcrops. At some spots the shrubs along the shore were cut away so they could take in the ocean views. After they crossed a bridge, the trail changed to hard packed dirt from pavement. They were glad to find this. Timothy sped up, taking the lead on the narrow path.

An hour into the run they stopped at a park bench overlooking the ocean to take in carbohydrates. Timothy had two peanut butter and jelly tortilla wraps in a plastic bag tucked into the back of his hydration vest. He took them out and handed one to Sandra.

"Thanks," she said.

Timothy ate two bites of his tortilla and spoke, "I'm starting to see things. I'm getting supernatural knowledge about complete strangers. Like Jesus was with the Samaritan woman at the well. Though it was his first time meeting her he knew she had been married five times before."

"Like with the woman at the well?"

"Yes, fellow travelers on the ship, I'm seeing things about them. Like with the guy I met on the track earlier today. I knew I needed to talk with him."

"How did you know?"

"It was like this inner voice, the Holy Spirit, spoke to me."

"Was it an audible voice?"

"No. More like a vision," Timothy replied, and finished eating the rest of his peanut butter and jelly tortilla wrap. He drank six gulps of fluid from one of the flasks in the front pouch of his hydration vest. "I think that's how we're going to find Moses' staff, with the help of the Holy Spirit."

Sandra stood up and started dynamic leg stretches, getting ready to run again. "Hopefully this antique dealer in Hamilton will be able to help us."

They ran for another hour following the Railway

Trail to the coast of North Shore Village. There they found an outdoor freshwater shower at a small beach where they could clean up. On the way to downtown Hamilton while walking in the midday sun, and the ocean breeze, they dried off. They reached the antique shop on Church Street just as Thomas and his two agents arrived.

The proprietor, an elderly man, welcomed them inside, introducing himself as Michael Miles. Speaking with a posh English accent he described the artwork and antiques on display. They mostly appeared to be related to Bermuda. Two glass enclosed cabinets contained worn artifacts that were found on sunken ships from the 1700's.

"Do you have any ancient items of Middle Eastern origin?" Thomas inquired.

"No," Michael replied. Pausing to think, he continued, "But there was a request related to that I received several months ago by e-mail. I considered it spam. As I recall, the person was searching for ancient Middle Eastern artifacts of Semitic origin."

"Do you still have the e-mail?" Thomas asked.

"It should be in my spam file. Let me have a look." He checked the computer next to the cash register. After clicking and scrolling through e-mails he found it. "Brilliant! It's still there. The signature block includes a phone number."

Sandra leaned over the counter to see the screen, saying, "Would it be possible to get a copy?"

"I can do that," Michael said, as he clicked the computer's mouse. His ink-jet printer beeped and printed out three pages. He passed them to Thomas, asking, "Is there anything else I can help you with?"

"No thank-you, this is perfect," Thomas said. "Have a great day."

Timothy, Sandra, Thomas and the two agents turned to head out the front entrance.

"I'd be forever in your debt if you would tell others about my shop," Michael bid them farewell.

Timothy turned back, saying, "Thanks, we will!"

They walked together down to the Hamilton Ferry Terminal feigning interest in the surroundings. The cruise ship was scheduled to depart that evening for Portugal. As they waited in line to purchase ferry tickets back to the Royal Naval Dockyard Pier, Thomas requested through a text message on his smart phone that a trace be made for the number found on the e-mail's signature block. A few minutes later someone in Washington confirmed they received it.

Due to the large crowd of fellow passengers boarding the cruise ship back at the pier, Timothy and Sandra lost sight of the FBI agents. They had agreed to meet with Thomas later that evening for dinner in the

Fifty's Diner. There was enough time to return to their cabin to get changed into tidy casual wear better suited for dining. Timothy was so hungry after their Bermuda Railway Trail run; he could hardly wait to sink his teeth into one of the delicious burgers the diner served.

Bermuda faded into the setting sun as the cruise ship headed east. Timothy took in the view from where he sat at the small round table in the Fifty's Diner with Sandra at his side. Satisfied with a good meal he placed his unused napkin on top of the empty plates in front of him.

Thomas was at a nearby table dressed in a loud Hawaiian shirt. He saw they were finished eating so he stood and came over to greet them, saying, "How're you two doing?"

"Good," Timothy replied.

"Care to join us in the lounge? I've got good news." Thomas smiled. He carried a cup of coffee.

"Sure," Sandra said, getting up.

On the deck outside the Fifty's Diner, they followed Thomas to the lounge area consisting of several sets of wicker furniture with plush cushions.

"So, what's the good news?" Timothy asked.

"We were able to trace the e-mail," Thomas continued, "to an IPS located in southeast Asia."

"Where, specifically?" Sandra pressed for more information. She chose a place to sit with a view of the horizon.

"From a super-yacht in the Arabian Sea. A web-based map of maritime traffic shows its transponder headed up the Suez Canal to the Mediterranean Sea two weeks ago."

Timothy nodded. "And that's where it is now?"

Thomas sipped his coffee and said, "Yes, and it's moving toward us. At its present rate of travel, it should be able to meet up with us in the port at Lisbon, Portugal. We're trying to get more information on the actual owners of the vessel. It takes some time as they use offshore shell companies to hide their identities. We believe they'll try to hand off the wooden staff there."

Timothy snuggled closer to Sandra in their sofa. "I'm glad that contact in Hamilton worked out," he said. The couple put their feet up on a wicker ottoman watching the last coral colored light on the horizon fade to black. The stars in the northern skies soon appeared.

Sandra hugged Timothy, saying, "Ahh! it's so beautiful."

Thomas finished drinking his coffee and stood up to leave. He turned back, remembering something he wanted to ask Sandra, "Oh, were you able to talk with any of the nurses?"

"Yes, the nurses working on board the cruise ship hold the rank of officers which provides them with special privileges like free access to the spas," Sandra replied. "That's where Timothy and I met three of them the other day. They ended up inviting us to the infirmary. I had many questions about the cases they handled daily. Common problems include cardiac emergencies, diabetes complications and stomach disorders. It didn't seem busy there. Most of the beds were empty."

Timothy added, "It's easy for us to stop by the infirmary as it's around a hundred meters away, down the hall from our cabin. Our new friends there are nurses; Debbie, Olivia and ..." he paused trying to recall the last name, "... and Judy."

"Well, keep checking to see if they're getting any unusual reports," Thomas said, turning to walk away. "Good night!"

#   #   #

Over the next three days Timothy and Sandra developed a routine for life on board the ship. This included early morning prayers and Bible reading in the cabin followed by exercise on the track and a visit with their new friends at the infirmary. They had lunches at the buffet where there was a healthy selection of fresh fruit and salads. Afternoons were spent on lounge chairs around the pools, reading or watching educational pod casts on their smart phones. The Italian restaurant on the eight floor offered a variety of broiled meats and pasta, so they ate suppers there.

They met other passengers and learned that most of them were on board the cruise in the pursuit of happiness. They wanted to make good memories sharing fun times with friends and family. For a few it was a chance to create a new identity, to no longer be known by an employee number, one who sits at a desk in a cubicle identical to so many others, following the same route to and from work, day after day.

Soon after the cruise ship passed the halfway point between Bermuda and Portugal, a repeated call over the public address system caught Timothy's attention. It had an urgent tone, requesting for those on board who were doctors or nurses to report to the infirmary. Timothy and Sandra both sat up from where they were reclining on deck chairs near one of the pools. They removed their earphones and looked to each other. Quickly gathering up their belongings, they headed straight for the infirmary.

They found nurses, Debbie, and Olivia, holding clipboards, performing triage on passengers. Some were in wheelchairs, others on gurneys, lined up in the reception area.

"What's wrong?" Sandra asked Olivia.

"They all have the same symptoms," Olivia replied, looking up, taking notes.

"What is it?" Sandra continued.

"Snake bites."

"What kind of snake?"

Olivia exposed the swelling bite mark on a casualty's leg. "That's what we're trying to find out."

Fighting convulsions, a teenage boy on a gurney weakly raised his hand, miming the movements of a cobra's head. Timothy noticed this and came closer to where the boy lay.

"Cobra? You were bit by a cobra?" Timothy asked in a whisper.

"Yes," the boy answered, and passed out.

Not wanting to cause more panic, Timothy went to find one of the doctors in the emergency ward to tell him they needed an anti-venom for Cobra bites.

"We have some," the doctor replied. He checked the medication fridge. "There's four vials."

"Good. But you'll need more," Timothy cautioned the doctor.

In the next room Timothy found three ship security staff, and Thomas, who had blueprints of the ship spread out on a table. Using information collected from the wounded they marked out where the bites occurred.

"The first bite happened on deck eleven toward the stern," Thomas said, using a yellow highlighter to mark the spot. "The next two were by the elevator halfway down the hall."

"We've got to try to contain this thing without causing panic," Marvin, the head of security addressed two of his senior staff. "Get ..."

Thomas interrupted Marvin, "Put out a PA to have everyone return to their cabins. They'll be safer there."

"And who are you?" Marvin grimaced.

"Thomas Bright, FBI," Thomas replied, flashing his ID badge.

Using the hand-held radio strapped to his belt, Marvin contacted the ship surveillance room. He asked them to make the on board emergency announcement.

"We need more anti venom too," Timothy addressed everyone in the room. "The ship's infirmary will run out soon. We'll need search and rescue to bring some from the mainland."

"We're in the middle of the Atlantic, search and

rescue is hours away," Marvin huffed, distressed. "What kind of snake are we dealing with anyway?"

"It's a king cobra," Timothy replied, "and if I can find it, I can stop it."

"You're crazy!" Marvin scoffed. "How?"

"This isn't just any cobra," Timothy explained. "It's a walking stick that's transformed into a snake. Did you ever read the Bible?"

Marvin looked confused. "Yes, when I was a kid."

"Well, remember when God turned Moses' staff into a snake?"

"Okay, yes," Marvin replied, growing impatient.

"The cobra on this ship used to be the staff Moses used."

"The same one?"

"Yes," Timothy continued, "and if I can get close enough to it, I'll be able to pick it up like Moses did."

"If you're sure about this, is there anything you need?"

Timothy thought, and asked, "Are there any large nets on board?"

Marvin wanted to know more. "Nets, like fishing nets?"

"Yes," replied Timothy, "large fish nets."

A senior security personnel member stepped forward, suggesting, "What about the volleyball nets? Would they work?"

Timothy and Thomas liked the idea.

"Those might," Timothy said. "Let's get them."

Radio chatter interrupted their conversation. Marvin listened to the caller on his headset. When it ended, he turned to Thomas, saying, "We've got to move. Passengers heading back to their cabins encountered the cobra on deck eight."

Sandra stayed behind at the infirmary to help the nurses while Timothy, Thomas, and two of the ship's security personnel, set out to search the ship for the snake. Their first destination was the sportsplex on deck eighteen where the volleyball nets were stored. With most of the passengers confined to their cabins they were able to move quickly through the network of halls to the elevator.

They met a few stragglers who Marvin urged to return to their cabins due to an on board emergency. An elderly couple, wearing swimsuits and sandals, appeared to be oblivious to the danger. The husband apologized, "Sorry, we didn't bring our hearing aids to the pool."

62

Inside the elevator there was an eerie silence as they headed up to the top deck. When the door opened, Thomas was the first to step out. He pointed to the pickle-ball court on the starboard side. "The sports storage room is over there."

They found the entrance down the hallway beside the basketball court. Marvin used his smart card to gain access. Inside there were two volleyball nets hung on hooks, fastened to a long shelf. Timothy glanced around the room to see if there was any other equipment they could use. There were lighter pickle ball nets and wooden boxes filled with basketballs and volley balls; nothing useful.

Two security personnel with them rolled the volleyball nets up to a size that was easy to carry under an arm, wrapping a bungee cord around each one to keep them tight.

"Is the snake still on deck eight?" Timothy asked Marvin.

"Yes," Marvin replied, checking a text message on his smart phone, "minutes ago the manager at the Italian restaurant spotted it."

They hurried back to the elevator. Thomas, walking next to Timothy, asked him, "Are you sure about this?"

"Yes, I believe we can stop it, but it will take a miracle," Timothy said, remembering the vow he made to

God on the mountain trail in Flagstaff about a week before this. "Are you a praying man?"

Thomas nervously laughed, "No."

"You better start to. You see, God is the architect of all. The seas, the skies, the earth, and every living thing on it was spoken into existence by God."

Thomas listened intently.

"Mankind was the pinnacle of God's creation. We're different from every other created thing. We're created in God's own image. Because of this we can talk to him, and he can talk to us," Timothy continued.

"I get it. Like an eagle can talk to another eagle because their made in the same image. Maybe I should start praying," Thomas conceded.

"Yes," replied Timothy. He took a deep breath before stepping into the elevator. "Let's go!" he hollered to the two security staff hauling the volleyball nets who hustled to join them.

Upon reaching deck eight the five men exited the elevator. They headed toward the Italian restaurant moving in a starboard direction up the hallway. On their left they passed an atrium open to deck six. An ornate glass chandelier made from a variety of long glass tubes hung from the centre of its ceiling.

"Wait in the hall with a net," Timothy told one of the ship security members, "in case the cobra comes out of the restaurant here." The hall was narrower there just after the double wooden doors to the Italian restaurant.

The manager heard their voices in the hall and came out of the office where she had taken shelter. She pointed to the bar at the far end of the room. "That's where I saw it," she spoke in a whisper.

Thomas understood. "Thanks. We'll catch it," he said. "Please stay in your office."

Alert to any movement the four of them crept toward the bar in a single file formation keeping low so they could check under the dining room tables.

Suddenly, a wine glass smashed, falling from one of the mirrored bar shelves.

They rushed forward. Timothy spotted the snake's tail slithering around the corner as it went past the swinging door into the kitchen.

"We've located the cobra!" Marvin spoke into the mic on his radio headset. "It's in the kitchen for the Italian restaurant on deck eight. Check the blueprints. How many exits are there?"

As Marvin waited for an answer Timothy and Thomas moved closer to the kitchen. "Get the volleyball net ready," Timothy said, motioning for the security personnel member to unhook the bungee. They spread the net out, leaning it over chairs near the kitchen door.

"This is the only exit," Marvin repeated what he heard over the radio, "but the kitchen does have laundry and garbage chutes leading to deck four."

"Who's going in to chase the cobra out?" Thomas asked, indicating that he was not the one who was going to volunteer.

There was a short silence.

"I'll go," Timothy said, "and if I can grab it, the cobra should turn back into a wooden staff."

Cautiously, Timothy entered the kitchen. As he stepped forward, he scanned the surface of the stainless steal cabinets and counters ahead for movement and bent down to check the floor. Two mixing bowls and some utensils were scattered across the tiles. There was something long and round in the corner under the fridge beside the gas stove. It was too dark to make out in the shadows. Was it part of the cobra? Timothy wondered.

Next to the fridge he crouched down on all fours. There was something there. Timothy was able to get his hand around it. He pulled. "I've got it!" Timothy shouted. Out from under the cabinet came a three-foot Genoa Salami. It looked fresh. "It's just a Salami!" Timothy sighed as he stood up. "The cobra's gone," he yelled so

Thomas and Marvin could hear, "It must've used the garbage or laundry chute."

"Deck four! Deck four!" Marvin called to security personnel on his radio headset. "Check the laundry and garbage sections for the cobra! We're on our way there."

Timothy huffed, and frowned, as he came back to join Marvin, Thomas, and the others, in the restaurant dining room. They quickly rolled up the volleyball nets and headed to the elevators.

A call came in from Sandra on Timothy's smart phone while the elevator was on the way down. Someone died in the infirmary. It was a wealthy older man who had offered to pay a million dollars for the last vile of anti venom. The doctors chose to treat the younger women and children first.

"Are search and rescue on the way with more?" Timothy asked Sandra.

"Yes," Sandra replied, "They're en route, but still hours from getting here."

"We think the cobra is on deck four. We're heading there now," Timothy concluded the call, saying, "I love you, take care."

Deck four was where most cruise ship staff had cabins. The crew cafeterias and recreational facilities were located there too. Exiting the elevator, they headed toward the stern through the main hallway. It was wide enough for a small forklift to do a three-point turn. The laundry and garbage wings were across from each other at the far end.

"How do we do this?" Thomas asked Timothy.

"Let's try to lure the cobra into the hallway. Have them hold the volleyball nets on both sides of the exits, there," Timothy explained, pointing to where the security staff and the agents should stand.

When everyone was positioned in the hall, Timothy and Marvin entered the laundry. Wheeled carts stacked high with white bedsheets and towels were lined up inside by the door. The huge washing machines and clothes dryers inside were turned off, abandoned by the crew. Piles of dirty laundry strewn around by them were evidence of their hasty departure. Along the stern wall four laundry chutes, jutting out from the ceiling, were opened directly above two large black bins.

"If the snake came down that way it would've landed there," Marvin said, nodding his head toward the chutes.

Timothy poked at the piles of sorted laundry on a stainless-steel table near the black bins. He watched and waited to see if there was any movement. Nothing moved.

Marvin surveyed the system of pipes and air ducts fastened to the ceiling above them. The cobra was not there.

It was then that Timothy spotted the cobra curled up on the second shelf of a three-shelf wheeled trolley.

"Cobra's can sense movement," Timothy told Marvin, "Rush to the exit with me when I say go."

"Okay," Marvin got ready to run.

"Go!" Timothy cried out, dashing to the exit. Marvin followed close behind.

The snake dropped from its perch when the men started to run, crossing fifteen meters in seconds. Out of the corner of his eye, Timothy could see it when he turned back. The cobra was close.

"Get ready!" Timothy shouted, as they burst through the swinging laundry room doors.

The ship security personnel, holding a volleyball net, jumped forward the moment the king cobra entered the hall. The snake became entangled in the net's black nylon cords, in a slithering rage, attempting to bite at those around. With its fangs caught, Timothy reached for the Cobra's tail, and when they touched there was a flash of light that knocked everyone to the deck floor. The cobra transformed into a walking stick. Timothy, flat on his back, grasped it with one hand.

Everyone scrambled to their feet with their eyes fixed on the ancient walking stick. Timothy stood up. He tapped the almond wood staff on the metal door frame. It sounded solid and looked like it had when he last saw it at the Harvard Museum of the Ancient Near East.

"Huh!" Timothy smiled. "It's back to normal." He glanced around. "We should head back to the infirmary."

"Amazing," Thomas replied. "Let's go."

On the way to the elevator Marvin radioed the surveillance control room informing them that the cobra was no longer a threat and that the on board emergency was over. A public address announcement sounded as they returned to the infirmary on deck thirteen. It was repeated three times saying, "Passengers are now free to leave their cabins as the on board emergency is resolved." Life on board the ship could return to its normal leisurely pace.

Timothy felt he should try to help the snake bite victims who were confined to hospital gurneys and wheelchairs at the infirmary waiting for a search and rescue flight to arrive. The doctors ran out of anti venom so there were some who were left untreated. Timothy went to those patients first. He prayed simple prayers over them as he lifted Moses' staff in his right hand. The branch of almond wood he grasped was just a point of contact for the highest power that existed in the universe.

"Look to the staff," Timothy spoke in a soothing voice to the patients. "Be healed in Jesus' name."

The atmosphere in the ICU became electric.

Marvin, Thomas, and the agents stood speechless, watching Timothy as he went to pray for those suffering. The victims' symptoms suddenly subsided. The convulsions and spasms left as they made eye contact with the wooden staff. When he was done, Timothy slumped to the floor, falling to his knees. The power of God flowing through him left him feeling drained. He rested.

After a few minutes Sandra entered the room and put her hand on Timothy's shoulder. "Wow!" Timothy said, turning to look up to his wife. She had tears in her eyes. Seeing smudges of mascara blotting the tops of her cheeks, he asked her, "What's wrong?"

"Nothing's wrong. They're healed," Sandra sobbed. "All of them are healed."

A miracle had occurred. Patients left the gurneys and wheelchairs, indicating to those around that they felt fine.

Timothy and Sandra spent the rest of the day in their cabin. They ordered dinner through room service and enjoyed a meat lovers pizza together. Timothy was fast asleep by eight-thirty, in bed not far from the walking stick. He was determined not to let it out of his sight.

In the middle of the night, they were woken by a knock on their cabin door. Timothy threw on a bath robe and went to see who it was. In the hall there were two soldiers dressed in black fatigues. They each wore helmets with night vision attachments and had assault rifles.

With the door opened slightly, Timothy asked, "What's going on?"

"We're Navy Seals, and we have orders to evacuate you and your wife from this vessel along with Moses' staff," one of the soldiers said with an authoritative tone in his voice.

Timothy noticed a group of ship security staff gathered further down the hall near the atrium. More Navy Seals were with them.

Sandra joined Timothy at their cabin door. "Okay, give us a couple of minutes to put on some clothes," she said, and shut the door.

In a flurry of activity Timothy and Sandra got dressed, searching their dresser drawers, grabbing jeans, t-shirts, and pullovers. The last item Timothy picked up was the wooden staff. He held it tightly as they exited the cabin. They were escorted down the hall by the Navy Seals, heading stern toward the elevators.

As they walked, Sandra asked a question, "Where are you taking us?"

"To an undisclosed location," was the reply. "But don't worry, you'll be safe."

They were led to the mini-golf course up on deck twenty where a Sikorsky Black Hawk helicopter hovered fifteen meters above the ship. A triangular harness was lowered to them on a hoist hook. Timothy offered to go first. A Navy Seal showed him how to put on the harness. Still grasping tightly to the walking stick, Timothy ascended. The wind caught him a couple of times and spun him around, but he kept going up. Once he was near the helicopter's open sliding door, the winchman helped him inside.

Sandra came up next.

With all the loud engine and hydraulic hoist noise drowning out the sounds of their voices Timothy and Sandra struggled to communicate. A crew member directed them to two seats. They sat down and fastened their seatbelts. Within minutes the crew offered them radio headsets with noise canceling earmuffs and mics so they could talk.

There was something familiar about the winchman seated across from them. When Timothy gave him a second look, he realized it was Enoch dressed in a dark gray flight suit and helmet with a built-in radio headset. The last time they had talked was at the Harvard University press conference. Enoch smiled at Timothy and winked.

While the helicopter flew across the Atlantic Ocean, through the cover of night, Enoch and Timothy conversed by radio headset.

"You're going to get through this. Everything will

be okay. Keep watch over the wooden staff," Enoch encouraged Timothy.

"Are you an angel?"

"No, I'm human, but I've been alive a long time."

"How long?"

"Since before the great flood. Noah was a relative. I never died. God took me up to heaven. Every now and then he sends me out on special missions like this one."

"So, you're like an angel?"

"In many respects, however, angels don't get to experience the joy of salvation like we do. They don't have a fallen nature."

"Where are we going?"

"Soon we'll be landing on an aircraft carrier anchored off the coast of Lisbon, Portugal."

#   #   #

Events went just as Enoch said. After the Black Hawk helicopter landed safely on the aircraft carrier flight deck, Timothy and Sandra were escorted inside the mammoth ship, down an elevator to one of the conference rooms where a delegation of CIA agents waited to debrief them. A couple of high-ranking officers where there too. It looked like they had been there for hours, making plans, seated around a long table scattered with laptops, note pads, and water bottles. Two plush office chairs were offered to Timothy and Sandra so they could sit at the far end of the table.

The highest-ranking officer in the room, a Lieutenant Colonel, started the debrief. He wore a Marine's cadpat uniform that displayed his rank but no name or unit patches. "Thank-you for being so co-operative to meet with us. Sorry that we had to wake you in the middle of the night but for operations like this we find it works best that way," he continued. "We've been following the FBI reports on the walking stick you found - its theft and recent recovery. This is much more than an ancient relic. I see you brought it with you."

"Yes. It never leaves my sight," Timothy replied as he set the wooden staff on the tabletop.

The Lieutenant Colonel got up from where he was seated and stepped closer to Timothy, putting on his reading glasses to examine the staff's engravings. "It truly is a miraculous relic of high value," he said, gazing at the branch of almond wood. "There's a nation that will stop at nothing to get control of this. They're the ones behind its theft. They are also the ones who have a super yacht moored in Lisbon waiting for your arrival so they can attempt to steal it again."

A middle-aged woman in a gray suit dress who sat next to Sandra spoke, introducing herself as a European

CIA operative. She shared her code name, Saturn. "We've got a plan to stop these people, but we'll need your help. The man on board the cruise ship who died after he was bitten by the cobra – the one who attempted to pay a million dollars for the last vile of anti venom – was the courier for Moses' staff. We've checked his smart phone records. He had no idea what he was carrying. To him it was just another high value smuggling job like others he had done before. We believe the real people behind this theft are in Lisbon."

Timothy understood. He could see where this was going, and asked, "So, what do you want me to do?"

Saturn hit a button on her laptop. A map flashed onto the high-definition screen fastened to the wall behind her. It showed a network of city streets in Lisbon near the port. She pointed to a spot along the bank of the Tagus River. "We want you to be part of a press conference announcing the recovery of Moses' Staff. We'll hold it at a UNESCO World Heritage Site, The Belem Tower, in two days. All appearances of high security will be hidden. It will look as though it was coordinated with the help of one of the local museums," Saturn explained.

"You'll be using the staff as bait," Timothy said.

"Precisely," Saturn replied. "If it looks like an easy theft and they decide to stay in port we could catch the thieves in the act."

Sandra leaned forward, and asked Saturn, "Will Timothy's life be in danger?"

Saturn shook her head. "No. They want the staff, not Timothy. To reduce the risk, we want to make a 3D copy of the relic and put that on display for the press conference. It would mean that we would have to take custody of the original for a few days."

Upon hearing this Timothy slid the walking stick from the conference tabletop down to his lap, grasping it with both hands, saying, "I don't think that's a good idea. I didn't choose the staff. The staff chose me. It's best to keep it in my possession until it can be returned to the Harvard Museum of the Ancient Near East."

For an uncomfortable amount of time the only sound in the room was of fingers typing on laptop keyboards. Eventually, the Lieutenant Colonel looked up to Saturn and said, "That shouldn't be a problem."

#   #   #

Before sunrise Timothy and Sandra were back on board the cruise ship, under blankets, inside their cabin. The quick mission to be debriefed on the aircraft carrier seemed like just a dream. Peace came to them, and they drifted off to sleep.

Late in the morning Sandra offered to watch the wooden staff for Timothy so he could go for a training run on deck seventeen. The one-hundred-mile mountain run that he planned to compete in was less than a month away. He needed to get in some intense running intervals.

Outside in the fresh ocean breeze Timothy ran for over two hours, stopping only to drink water and to do some dynamic stretches. He prayed at times, committing his concerns about the upcoming press conference to the Lord, hoping that the CIA would have everything organized. Though they would not be the only ones working behind the scenes. Timothy was aware of how God's angels were working too.

Thomas arranged for a private dinner that night, catered by the Fifty's Diner, where Timothy and Sandra, could join him to discuss the plans for the next day without interruption. They met on deck eight in a small, enclosed dining room.

Once everyone was seated, Timothy said a little prayer under his breath and began eating his favorite cruise ship burger and fries. After a couple of bites, he thanked Thomas for the invitation.

"Thank you both for all your help," Thomas replied. "It's a little celebratory dinner for us. We recovered the staff, and it will soon be returned to its rightful place."

They did a cheer for the ancient relic with raised glasses of soda.

"Have you heard anymore about what will happen tomorrow?" Timothy asked Thomas.

"Yes. The Belem Tower in Lisbon will provide a display case for Moses' staff like the one where it was kept at Harvard, with double locks, and it's alarmed. When we disembark the ship at the Lisbon Port a Portuguese delegation will meet us at the jetty. We'll be taken by buses to the tower. At ten-hundred-hours the press conference is scheduled to start."

Sandra had a couple of questions, and asked, "Who knows about this?"

Thomas paused to think for a second, to give the best answer. "The whole world knows. International press will be there. Fortunately, The Belem Tower is like a mousetrap. At high tide it can only be accessed by a bridge. There will be security on that to monitor all who come and go."

Nodding, Sandra continued, "So, anyone could be there?"

"Yes, the public will be given access along with the press. If a wealthy Arabian oligarch wanted to get a closer look at the staff that will be the perfect time to do it. But don't worry, Timothy will be safe. No one with a weapon will be able to get near the Belem Tower."

Thomas said that on that day their luggage would be moved by agents from the cruise ship to a hotel in Lisbon. Their arranged return to America was by commercial aircraft. If all went as planned, they would be back home in Arizona by the end of the week.

The next day Timothy and Sandra disembarked from the cruise ship along with the other passengers at the port in Lisbon. Buses waited in the parking lot to shuttle them to The Belem Tower. Timothy carried Moses staff in his right hand. A small backpack was slung over his shoulders containing his wallet, passport, note pad and smart phone. At the end of the jetty was a building they had to pass through to get to the parking lot. A sign above the entrance said in several languages that it was the office for Portugal customs and immigration. Inside, six officers at three control gates checked passports and questioned foreigners. The process ran smoothly. After twenty minutes they were out to the buses. Two men dressed in blue suits noticed Timothy carrying the walking stick. One was the curator of Lisbon's Calouste Gulbenkian Museum, Joseph Miranda. The other man was his assistant, Filipe Miguel.

"Welcome to Lisbon," Joseph greeted Timothy and Sandra shaking their hands directing them to step inside the nearest bus. "We work for one of the museums sponsoring this press conference. I see you hand carried the ancient relic with you."

"Yes," Timothy replied. "I know it's priceless, but I feel it's safest place is with me."

Joseph led Timothy and Sandra to the back of the bus to where an empty rectangular glass enclosed display case was laid out on the last row of seats. Its varnished mahogany base was about three inches thick.

"We had this made for you. It's suitable for this sort of item. The glass is bulletproof. It's alarmed, has a GPS tracker chip, and double locks. I have one key and my assistant has the other one required to open it," Joseph explained as he demonstrated the procedure. "The case has some weight and takes two people to carry."

With the display case open, Timothy set Moses' staff inside on a soft, rectangular, black velvet pad. Filipe closed the lid and locked one side with his key.

Joseph checked his watch. "We should leave now. The press conference starts in half-an-hour," he said, motioning with his hand to the bus driver.

The drive followed city streets that ran alongside the Tagus River. They passed dockyards and warehouses heading west on Infante Dom Henrique Avenue. After going under a suspension bridge the bus merged with traffic onto Brasilia Avenue.

Timothy pointed to a park beside a wharf were hundreds of yachts and sailboats were moored. "We must be getting close," he said to Sandra who was seated at his side.

The river water's surface sparkled in the morning light. Timothy watched a yacht as it left the shelter of the marina, sailing past a huge monument to Henry the Navigator, built in 1920 to mark 500 years since his death. In the distance he saw the Belem Tower. As they drove closer the presence of international press became apparent. Up ahead media vans and various national news network semi trucks with satellite up-links were parked at the edge of the road.

Pulling into the lot near The Belem Tower they spotted Thomas who had reserved a parking spot for them. Timothy took a deep breath as he thought about what he had to do. After the vehicle stopped, the bus driver opened the side exit door. Joseph thanked him.

Thomas came to help Timothy carry the staff and the display case through the park, over the bridge to the tower where hundreds of reporters, videographers, archaeologists, and others waited. Joseph and Filipe walked ahead of them, clearing the way so they would have an unobstructed route to the speaker's podium located at the far end of The Belem Tower's spacious courtyard. A long wooden table was there. They carefully set the display case on the center of it as photographers and cameramen jockeyed to get a good shot of the relic.

Timothy removed his backpack and took out his note pad. He quickly checked the notes that he wrote and placed them on the plexiglass lectern. Joseph showed Timothy how to work the mic at the podium beside it.

Joseph introduced himself and welcomed everyone. "I am the curator for Lisbon's Calouste Gulbenkian Museum. We are privileged to be one of the sponsors for todays' press conference, to share in bringing to the world this good news. Timothy Han is here to give you the details, and to answer your questions."

Timothy cleared his throat as he stepped behind the mic. He started off, saying, "Members of the press, archaeologists, and museum curators, we welcome you here today. We have good news indeed. Yes. Moses' staff was stolen in a highly organized theft nine days ago while it was being shipped to the Penn State Museum. We've been on a pursuit of it since then on a journey that took us from Flagstaff Arizona to New York City, the island of Bermuda, and on to the Atlantic coast just west of Portugal." He motioned with his hand toward the display case. "As you can see, we have recovered it." While Timothy spoke, he recognized the reporter, Jane Katz, seated in the second row. "Do any of you have questions?"

Along with many other reporters, Jane Katz raised her hand. Timothy let her ask the first question.

Jane stood. "There was a freak hailstorm in Pennsylvania and a strange outbreak of pestilence in New York recently, is there a connection between those events and the theft of the staff?" she asked.

"Yes," Timothy replied, "we believe that Moses' staff was present in both those incidences."

Jane pressed for clarification. "So, what you're saying is that Moses' staff still has the power it had in biblical times?"

Timothy hesitated before answering, "No, what I'm saying is that the God who chose to use Moses' staff, as a point of contact, still has the same power he had in biblical times."

Jane smiled. She understood and sat down.

Over the next fifteen minutes Timothy answered questions from more of the press gathered there. Several of them wondered if the strange phenomena that occurred around the staff could be explained by a series of odd coincidences. Timothy disputed this explanation. As he did, out of the corner of his eye, Timothy noticed a light gray colored Super Yacht heading down the river, approaching the tower. It had five decks and a helipad on its bow where a gray Bell helicopter sat. Thomas saw it too. He signaled for Timothy to end the news conference. The super yacht was the one owned by the Arabian oligarch.

Timothy motioned with his hand for Joseph to come up to the podium. He whispered something to him.

"Thank-you all for coming today," Joseph abruptly dismissed the crowd. "You are welcome to join us at the four-o-clock reception in the Calouste Gulbenkian Museum later today."

As the behemoth super yacht got closer, Timothy and Thomas picked up the wooden staff in its display case. They took it to one of the parked buses. Sandra followed close behind.

When the super yacht was only a couple of hundred meters away from the tower, Timothy clearly saw a man standing on its top deck who had binoculars. Strangely, the yacht didn't slow, but continued past the tower, moving at fifteen knots, down the river out toward the Atlantic Ocean. Timothy watched it go, seated on the bus next to Moses' staff.

Thomas and his assistant left Belem Park in a separate bus. Before going he told Timothy to stay with Joseph and Filipe at the Calouste Gulbenkian Museum until the afternoon reception there was over. He said they were picking up radio chatter which seemed to indicate that the whole crew and passengers on board the Arabian oligarch's super yacht had suddenly come down with a highly contagious skin rash with boils. They were refused entry into the country by Portugal customs and immigration. Thomas believed, for the time being, those on board the vessel were no longer a threat.

Timothy and Sandra felt elated when they heard the news, like a weight was suddenly lifted from them.

"Thank-you God!" Timothy cried out, slapping Sandra's hand.

The bus pulled out of the parking lot and headed toward the center of Lisbon to where the Calouste Gulbenkian Museum was located. The hotel where they would be spending the night was near there too. Most of the buildings they passed along the way had a similar look with five storeys and colorfully framed windows. Some of the narrow side streets were steep; so steep they had built funiculars to ascend. Timothy thought these streets would be a challenge to run up. He wondered if there would be time in their schedule to try. He made a mental note of the neighbourhood's location.

The low profile and minimalist design of the Calouste Gulbenkian Museum was a surprise to Timothy. It was not what he had imagined for a museum located in Lisbon, Portugal, with its modern, pristine water garden, well trimmed lawns, and manicured shrubbery. When the bus dropped them off at the front entrance, Sandra helped Timothy to carry the display case, with Moses' staff enclosed, into the museum. Filipe offered to take Sandra's place, but she insisted on carrying it all the way inside.

The reception for the international press wasn't scheduled to start until four-o-clock. Timothy and Sandra had time to explore the museum at a leisurely pace. They walked the halls, taking in the exhibits of ancient art from various parts of the world. Timothy kept Moses staff on hand. When they returned to the reception area near the entrance, they found caterers there who had set out tables with an assortment of finger foods and desserts. Filipe gave instructions to the servers showing them where to place the refreshments.

Timothy decided to return the staff to its display case and made sure it was locked. He left it there for the duration of the reception, doing interviews near it with international press. Sandra engaged in polite small talk with professors, archaeologists, and journalists, sipping punch, nibbling finger food.

Jane Katz with her videographer in tow found Timothy. She asked if he would mind answering a few questions on camera. He agreed to, so she had her production assistant clip a small mic onto the lapel of Timothy's shirt.

"I'm here in Lisbon, Portugal, with Timothy Han who discovered Moses' staff in Jordan earlier this year. We are getting reports from around the world of great church growth since the discovery of Moses' staff. How do you feel about that?"

"It's exciting to hear. I'm glad that I could play a small part in this," Timothy answered, "It humbles me too because Moses' staff found me. My life was changed by finding the staff just like the news of its existence has caused many around the world to re-examine their faith and experience revival. They have a healthy fear of God now."

"How has your life changed, exactly?"

"I used to rely on my own abilities and will power to deal with the challenges I faced in life. Since surrendering myself to the power of the new covenant in the blood of Jesus Christ I've gained a new strength. I'm no longer on my own trying to make things happen."

"New covenant in the blood of Jesus Christ, what's that?"

"If you read the Bible from cover to cover, you'll see that covenant is essentially what it is all about. God wanted to form a relationship with mankind, and he chose to do that by making a covenant with us. It started with Abraham under the old covenant and was completed by Jesus Christ under the new covenant."

"So, what we know as the Old Testament and New Testament could be called the old covenant and the new covenant. Is there anything else you would like to add?"

"Yes, I think understanding God's covenant with mankind is the key to discovering your individual destiny," Timothy concluded.

Jane Katz pondered Timothy's last comment. She took a deep breath and leaned closer to him saying with the camera off, "Thank-you. I needed to hear that."

Timothy smiled at her. "I know."

The highlight of the afternoon for Timothy was when Thomas gifted him with a custom-made black leather storage tube for Moses' staff. It had a zippered end and padded shoulder straps. As the reception ended Thomas approached Timothy and Sandra with a long box wrapped in silver paper. "In appreciation of all your help in this mission we had this made for you," Thomas said, handing the package to Timothy.

"Thank-you!" Timothy replied. He tore the wrapping apart.

Applause erupted from the reception guests when they saw what the gift was.

Early, the next morning, the hotel concierge gave Timothy directions to a running trail that led through meadows and forests up the peak of mount Monsanto. The trail-head was an easy two kilometers run away through the narrow, hilly, Lisbon streets he had spotted the previous day from the taxi. He left a note in the hotel suite for Sandra telling her of his whereabouts. She was still fast asleep and would most likely not wake up until he was finished his run. He left the walking stick on the floor at the foot of the bed inside its new custom-made leather storage tube.

Timothy had to be careful on the steep city streets as the worn tiles on the sidewalk were slippery with morning dew. He wore his favorite running shorts along with his hydration vest and a t-shirt. Being outside so early it felt cool. The dawn air had a chill. Upon reaching the start of the forest trail to Monsanto Timothy was warmed up. He ran for a good hour before turning around near the top. There, he had a great view of the sunrise silhouetted against the clouds on the east horizon.

The descent was quick. The evergreen trees he passed reminded him of the ones on the trails in Flagstaff. Birds chirped in the highest branches warming their feathers in the morning sunlight. Halfway down, Timothy felt the urge to pray. Like usual he covered his wife, asking God to bless her and to keep her safe. He prayed for Thomas and the other CIA agents that they would succeed in catching the Arabian oligarch.

Entering the city center streets of Lisbon there were cars to contend with. Nearing the hotel Timothy heard honking horns. Commuters coming and going to work filled the narrow lanes. Timothy waited for a streetcar to pass before he crossed the road to his hotel. The run was completed in just over two hours. Like he had planned he stayed on pace.

Strangely, the door to their hotel room was open. Sandra wasn't there. Clothing was strewn about in a haphazard manner. The walking stick and its leather storage case was gone.

"Sandra!" Timothy cried out, as he checked inside the bathroom. "Sandra!" he called down the hall.

He remembered the smart phone he had tucked into one of the pockets of his hydration vest. Timothy swiped it on and called Sandra's phone. It rang. Her smart phone was on the floor in the hotel room plugged into a wall socket, charging. Sandra and the wooden staff were gone.

Timothy took the elevator four floors down to the lobby. He rushed to the reception desk.

The manager saw that he was about to panic. "Can I help you sir?" he asked.

"I'm looking for my wife?" Timothy said, scrolling through photos saved on his smart phone. He found a clear one of Sandra. "She looks like this."

The manager adjusted his reading glasses to see the photo better. "No," he sighed. "But I just came on for the day shift ten minutes ago." The manager looked up over Timothy's shoulder. Sandra was there, crossing the lobby coming out of the restaurant where a breakfast buffet was being served. "Sir, there she is," he said, pointing with his finger.

Timothy turned around and saw Sandra. She was dressed for the day and had the leather storage tube for the walking stick slung over one shoulder. He ran to embrace her, saying, "I'm so glad to see you!"

Sandra pushed her sweaty husband away. "You need a shower."

"Our hotel room was broken into. They did it while you were down here having breakfast. When I returned from my run, I found that you and the staff were missing. I thought …"

Sandra interrupted him, saying, "We should contact Thomas."

They went up in the elevator.

Thomas answered their call on the second ring. He told them to leave the hotel for the airport as they could be in danger.

Back at their room Sandra retrieved her smart phone. She chose an outfit for Timothy from the clothes scattered around. "Take a quick shower, and then put this on," she said, pushing Timothy toward the bathroom. "You stink."

Timothy had a quick shower and got dressed. They grabbed what they could easily carry from their hotel room and left to the main lobby. The concierge there arranged a taxi for them. Timothy recognized two CIA agents who showed up at the hotel just as they were leaving. The agents made sure that the couple found transportation with Moses' staff safely accompanying them inside its leather storage tube.

Thomas met up with Timothy and Sandra at the Humberto Delgado Airport terminal two where passengers flying private aircraft had a separate luggage check-in area and lounge. He had three agents with him who wore radio headsets and frag vests. They were armed with pistols.

Thomas greeted them and asked, "Did the thieves get away with anything?"

"They took my notepad. I was using it as a journal," Timothy replied.

As Timothy and Sandra were quickly ushered through security, Thomas explained, "There's been a change in the plans due to the new threat level. Your return flight to America will be on board a private jet, an FBI Gulfstream, with us. A stop will be made in Boston so you can return the wooden staff to the Harvard Museum of the Ancient Near East."

"It will be good to see Professor Van Mappen again," Timothy remarked, as he and Thomas chatted.

"They have upgraded their security and hired additional staff," Thomas explained.

Timothy took off his backpack and set it in a plastic tray before the x-ray machine. He held onto the walking stick and went through the metal detector, saying, "That's where Enoch said it should be kept so there is the best place for it."

Thomas laughed. "Enoch? I still haven't met that guy."

"The last time I talked with him was on the Blackhawk helicopter that evacuated us from the cruise ship. He was part of the crew, a winchman."

"Did he tell you his last name?"

"No."

After waiting in the departures lounge ten minutes a

bus came to collect them to transit them to where the FBI Gulfstream jet was parked on the flight line. Once Timothy and Sandra were inside, and the door was closed, they felt safe. They could rest after enduring a traumatic morning of being robbed and in danger.

The Gulfstream G650 interior was almost like the one in the FBI jet they flew from Flagstaff. This one, however, had an extra row of seating and a sofa near the entrance instead of a desk with computer monitors. Including Timothy and Sandra fifteen passengers and two flight attendants were on board. Thomas sat across from them in one of the plush leather seats as the plane took off. He looked tired.

Timothy reclined his seat and drifted off to sleep when the Gulfstream reached cruising altitude. He woke up as dinner was being served. They were over the Atlantic Ocean with Boston still three hours away. The flight attendant offered Timothy the choice between chicken Parmesan or sirloin steak. He chose the chicken. Feeling groggy, he asked for a cola to drink.

"Thanks," Timothy said, as he sat forward and flipped up the small table inserted under his seat's left armrest. "I'm hungry."

Sandra had the sirloin with mushrooms and small potatoes. She smiled at Timothy after taking the first bite of steak. "This is nice!"

"The honeymoon continues," Timothy laughed.

After dinner Timothy called Professor Van Mappen to inform him that they were on their way to Boston with Moses' staff and that they would be there by two-thirty.

The plane touched down in Boston's Logan International Airport mid afternoon. Professor Van Mappen and two police officers met Timothy and Sandra as they exited arrivals. Timothy carried Moses' staff in its leather storage tube. He felt hesitant to pass it off to the professor but knew that was what God wanted.

"I have to take a look at it," Professor Van Mappen said, his eyes wide with excitement after he took hold of it.

"Go ahead," Timothy replied, "There's a zipper on the end."

The professor carefully opened the leather storage tube and pulled out the ancient relic. "Ah, beautiful, just like I remember it." The smooth almond wood glowed, reflecting the bright interior airport lights. "Thank-you so much for your assistance in retrieving this."

"You're welcome." Timothy was sad to see it go. "Well, I have an ultra marathon race to run next week. The FBI Gulfstream is refueling on the flight line now and will be departing soon. They're taking us back to Flagstaff, Arizona."

"We'll keep in touch," Professor Van Mappen said,

shaking Timothy's hand.

"Definitely," Timothy replied.

Professor Van Mappen and the security personnel turned and walked away. Timothy and Sandra watched the trio until they exited the arrivals hall and safely got into a waiting armored vehicle with two police car escorts. Timothy trusted that they would return to the museum without an incident.

\#   \#   \#

Back in Flagstaff Timothy had a week left in his training schedule to put in a couple of long runs. After that he would start his taper, resting up his body before the big race in California, the Western States 100. Some of the top ultra runners in the world would be there. The previous year Timothy had finished the race in the top ten, so he was given the opportunity to have an automatic entry for the next year. Thousands of runners qualify for the race every year but only three-hundred-and-sixty-nine are ever selected. Timothy felt honored to have another chance to race in the Western States 100.

Matt Carling came up to Flagstaff from Phoenix to train on the long runs with Timothy. Western States 100 allowed for a pacer to join runners on the later stages of the race. The plan was for Matt to be Timothy's. Before that he would help to serve at aid stations along with Sandra. Usually, the weather was hot on race day. The aid stations provided hydration drinks, ice, high carbohydrate snacks, first aid and encouragement for participants.

On the Wednesday of the big training week Timothy and Matt put in a six-hour run around the mountain trails of Flagstaff. This included nearly twelve thousand feet of elevation gain. Timothy's quad muscles were stiff and burning by the time that they finished. Sandra helped to massage out the pain in them at night before they slept. She told Timothy that she had found a church in Flagstaff she wanted to attend on Sunday. It was near their home in a forested area. They use the site of a summer camp that went out of business. The pastor was a trail runner.

When they went there, they found the church congregation had around a hundred attendees. The old log cabin lodge where they met felt cramped. Everyone was dressed casually. The pastor was tall and lanky with the solid physique of a veteran trail runner. He had on a pair of old jeans and a t-shirt he was awarded after finishing one of the local running races. He came to greet Timothy and Sandra. "Welcome, I'm Pastor Ned," he said, "I heard you were in town." He recognized them from recent news stories he had seen run by the local media. "I think we're going to have to get a bigger church."

"I can see," Timothy agreed.

Ned smiled as he continued, "There's a growing fear of God in this community. It started after we heard about the discovery of Moses' staff. The reports of supernatural signs and wonders - when the secular news ran the stories as factual events, I think it woke people up, and changed them."

"I know," Timothy replied, "It definitely changed me."

"This is your first time here. Would you be open to sharing your testimony in our meeting today after we worship?" Ned asked.

Timothy thought for a few seconds. He hadn't ever spoken to a church group. He felt peace about doing it though, so he said, "Sure. But I haven't ever preached before."

"Don't worry, we're very informal here. Just talk to us like you would to a friend if he was sitting across the table from you in a coffee shop."

"I can do that," Timothy agreed.

The adventures he had experienced in the pursuit of the stolen walking stick were still fresh in Timothy's mind. After a time of worship, led by a band with a young lady keyboardist, middle-aged drummer and two young men on electric guitars, Timothy was invited up to the lectern by Pastor Ned.

"Thank-you. As many of you already know, my wife, Sandra, and I, recently worked with the FBI and CIA to recover Moses' staff which was stolen by international, well financed, thieves. I can assure you the reports you heard about the supernatural phenomena that occurred are true. Seeing it firsthand has changed my life. I used to live by the strength of my own will power. Since I found Moses' staff I came to understand, and believe, that there is a much greater power at work in the world, and it's God's. I am learning about the new covenant He made with mankind which allows us to work with God, no longer relying on our own abilities but relying on his." Timothy went on to talk about how Jesus Christ had made a way for mankind to enter this covenant relationship with God through his own death on a cross. The covenant was sealed with his own blood. "I know I still have a lot to learn about this. I can say I've benefited already from God's strength working in my life. Once I came to the place of surrendering my will and heart to him," Timothy concluded.

Some people in the congregation shouted, "Amen!" Others had applause.

Timothy went to sit next to Sandra on one of the wooden pews near the back of the sanctuary. She patted Timothy's leg saying, "That was great!"

The pastor encouraged his congregation to keep Timothy in their prayers as he would be racing in the Western States 100 the next week.

# # #

The night before the race Timothy didn't get much sleep. With a 5 a.m. start in Olympic Valley he was up two hours before, inside their ski lodge motel room, eating a stack of pancakes. He drank some coffee and kept sipping on a bottle of water. Sandra double checked the contents of his hydration vest to make sure Timothy had enough to get him to the first aid station at Lyon Ridge, a ten-mile stage, with an elevation gain of two-thousand-five-hundred-and-fifty feet in the first four-and-a-half miles. The terrain on the summit was wilderness with patches of snow and streams to cross. In sections the trail was marked with pink ribbons tied to tree branches.

With all his gear on Timothy made his way down to the start ten minutes before the gun went off. He tucked into a place near the front pack runners recognizing some of the other elite racers gathered there. A couple of runners were minimalists, wearing just shorts and shoes with a hand carried bottle. Most of the participants had on hydration vests and hats. Unlike years before, he felt a peace, like this was where he belonged. He thought over his plan for the race and said a little prayer.

Part of the excitement found in running the Western States 100 were the elements of risks the course presented. Much of it wound through remote wilderness. It had rivers and streams to cross, hot dusty canyons and steep switchbacks that pounded at the quads for miles and miles. Suffering was unavoidable. The challenge had to be embraced. The winners were the ones who could ultimately persevere.

The racers counted down the last ten seconds, ready to sync their GPS watches. Upon reaching one, a shot gun was fired. They started off with a chorus of hoots and hollers. Some of the slower runners near the back of the pack held up their smart phone cameras taking in the scene as they jogged past the cramped starting gate.

Dawn light flashed across the snow-capped peaks above the runners as they made their way up the steep switchback logging road to Emigrant Pass. Timothy stayed with the chase pack, jockeying between fifteenth and eighteenth place. He was over the summit fifty minutes into the race and felt rested. The uneven condition of the trail was a challenge for the next few miles with Timothy having to keep up his pace while balancing his way through snow drifts, mud, and melt water. He stayed close to a couple of European runners entering the Lyon Ridge aid station with them.

Timothy felt encouraged to know he would see Sandra and Matt at the mile thirty Robinson Flat aid station. They had rented a four-wheeler so he figured they wouldn't have a problem making it across the logging roads to gain access. The thought of them waiting there made the miles feel shorter.

There were snow accumulations along the way, under the shade of the evergreens that flanked the trail. The warmth of the late Spring sun still had work to do. In fifteenth place for over an hour Timothy felt content. He kept the next runners ahead in his sights and was patient knowing that if he could keep enough strength reserved, he would be able to race for a top ten spot after the sixty-mile mark.

Timothy entered the Robinson Flat aid station four hours and thirty-two minutes into the race. He looked strong, and was smiling, when he saw Sandra at the side of the trail with filled hydration bottles, gels, bars, a tube of anti-chaffing cream, and dry socks laid out on a blue tarp.

"You're looking good!" Matt said, giving Timothy a high five.

"I feel good. There's more snow up her than last year."

"Do you need anything else?" Sandra asked after replacing the flasks in his hydration vest.

"Yes, more salt tablets, please, and a scarf," Timothy huffed, giving Sandra a plastic pill case to refill. "Thanks."

With his supplies replenished Sandra gave Timothy a kiss on the cheek, and he departed. The stop was less than two minutes, but Timothy felt it was enough of a boost to get him through the next eight miles until he would see them again at the Dusty Corners aid station. He left Robinson Flat in fourteenth position, a minute ahead of the next runner.

Timothy ran on from a place of rest. Peace was in his heart. He prayed, knowing he wasn't alone. The runner in thirteenth place stayed in his sights.

At Dusty Corners he did a quick exchange to get fresh hydration bottles and some crushed ice in his scarf as he would be heading into the hot canyons for twelve miles of steep descending switchbacks. He gained another place there. The European runner ahead of him sat down in the shade to change his socks and shoes.

"See you at Michigan Bluff!" Timothy called out to Sandra as he left.

The temperature change was abrupt. Timothy began to sweat heavily moving through the canyons. He stopped a couple of times to quickly soak his hat in the creeks by the trail dousing his head with cold water. The steep ascent after passing over a swinging footbridge slowed Timothy to power hiking mode. He couldn't run. After an hour and a half of running the ice in his scarf was gone. It was soaked with sweat. Both of his hydration bottles were empty. Timothy figured the El Dorado Creek aid station was half an hour away. He could make it there without cramping up if he slowed down. Just then he spotted what appeared to be a miracle; water coming out of a rock at the trailside.

There was enough of a fountain to refill his soft flask hydration bottles. "Thank-you God!" Timothy cried out.

Refreshed, Timothy picked up his running pace. The eleventh-place runner was not far away. Timothy quickly gained on him, and passed him a mile before El Dorado Creek. He was a fellow American runner nick named Ritz, who Timothy had raced in the past. He got the nick name Ritz in college because he had the habit of wearing a bow tie and tuxedo shirt in certain race events to try and psych out the competition.

"Are you okay?" Timothy asked him as he passed.

"I ran out of water," Ritz huffed.

"Here," Timothy said, turning back. He passed Ritz one of his half full hydration flasks. "Take it. I've got more."

Ritz took three deep gulps from the flask as Timothy sped ahead. "Thanks!" he hollered.

Sandra and Matt prepared for Timothy's arrival at Michigan Bluff. He came running around the corner, surprising them. He was five minutes ahead of what they had estimated.

"You're moving well," Sandra greeted him.

"I feel good," Timothy said, rubbing some anti chafing cream on the inside of both his thighs.

Sandra gave Timothy two new full hydration flasks, saying, "Tenth place. Good job. Can you keep it up?" She stuffed two carbohydrate gels in his vest pouch as Matt squeezed out a sponge of ice-cold water over Timothy's head.

"I can do it." Timothy smiled, and turned to run away.

Sandra waved to him, shouting, "See you at Forest Hill!"

As he ran, Timothy took two salt tablets washing them down with gulps of hydration fluid. The midday heat had arrived. A good portion of the next section of trail followed alongside a paved road where Matt joined Timothy as his pacer on the way into Forest Hill. A couple of professional videographers were set up there taking footage for documentary of the race. That's where they heard the news that one of the racers in the lead had dropped out due to severe leg cramps near green gate after the river crossing. Timothy felt encouraged knowing that he was now in ninth place.

Crowds of spectators were seated around the aid stations at Forest Hill. They cheered for Timothy and Matt as they left heading toward the long winding descent that would eventually lead them to the Rucky Chucky river crossing.

The eighth-place runner, a resident of France named Lennie, ran with Timothy and his pacer for two miles. They crossed the river together sharing the same raft and both chose to soak in the cool shallow water near the riverbank before pressing on. With a little over twenty miles to go they both had reserves of strength.

The last aid station where they planned to meet Sandra was at Green Gate. From there, she would go on to Auburn's Placer High School to wait for Timothy at the finish.

Timothy had gained two minutes on Lennie by the time that he reached Pointed Rocks. He flew through the aid station stopping for less than a minute to refill one flask and take a couple of salt tablets. As he left a race official told Timothy he was close to the runner in sixth place, a young American guy named Gordy who had gained an entry to the Western States 100 by winning a hundred mile ultra on the east coast earlier that year. They awarded him with a golden ticket.

Timothy pressed his running pace to close the gap. With six miles left in the race he did seven-minute miles all the way to No Hands Bridge. His pacer struggled to keep up. He spotted Gordy power hiking up a steep embankment two hundred yards ahead. Timothy was able to catch him after that on two miles of narrow switchback trails.

When Timothy reached Robie Point on the edge of Auburn at sunset he knew he was going to have a strong finish. He figured that if he could make it the next mile without any problems it would be a personal best time, he estimated it would be about seventeen hours and twenty minutes.

Running through the residential streets of Auburn Timothy passed crowds of cheering locals in lawn chairs. On the last stretch of road leading to the finish at the Placer High School race track Sandra joined Timothy running along beside him until he reached the gate at the sports field. Cheering fans in stands rose to their feet urging Timothy to finish strong. Encouraged with the adrenaline rush this brought on Timothy picked up his pace. He realized at this time why he liked to run so much. It was the closest he could get to flight. As he crossed the finish line the clock fastened to the banner above him read seventeen hours and twenty minutes, exactly.

A group of photographers and videographers turned their cameras toward Timothy as his finishing medal was placed around his neck. He hugged the official who did it. He hugged his wife. He thanked God. Timothy shook hands and gave high fives to those around him as he was led to a seat outside the recovery tent where he could rest. Race volunteers brought him a drink and a towel. He waited there to greet the next two runners that finished.

Later, Sandra massaged Timothy's legs as he lay on a cot inside the recovery tent. He there for a couple of minutes when he received a call on his smart phone. It was Jane Katz.

"Timothy, Sorry to bother you. I know you just finished a big race, but I've got some sad news," she said. "Moses' staff is gone."

"What?" Timothy said, slowly pulling himself up. "Stolen again?"

"No, it wasn't stolen," Jane explained. "It vanished. Video surveillance shows it just disappeared. All you see is a white light that flashes through the display case where it was kept. And then it's gone."

"That's not sad news," Timothy said, lying back down. "Someone from heaven came to take it, but don't worry Enoch told me there was a plan for it."

"What sort of plan?" Jane asked.

Timothy tried to remember Enoch's exact words. "He said there would be a new Exodus."

"A new Exodus?"

"Yes, they need it for a new Exodus."

"When's that going to happen?"

"Soon," Timothy concluded the call. "Thanks for letting me know. I appreciate that. I'm tired. I've got to get some rest." Timothy set his smart phone down and closed his eyes. Sandra continued to massage his legs. He soon was fast asleep.

9 798211 576001